MW01126471

THE PROTECTIVE WARRIOR

Navy SEAL Romance

CAMI CHECKETTS

Birch River Publishing

COPYRIGHT

The Protective Groom: Navy SEAL Romance

Copyright © 2018 by Cami Checketts

All rights reserved.

No part of this book may be reproduced in any form or by any electronic or mechanical means, including information storage and retrieval systems, without written permission from the author, except for the use of brief quotations in a book review.

DEDICATION

Thank you to the men and women who serve our country and protect life, liberty, and the pursuit of happiness.

CHAPTER ONE

CHANNING "RIVER" Duncan leaned back in his chair. The hobnob party was wrapping up and most of the celebrities and politicians had filtered out. River had been pleasantly surprised when Sutton Smith, billionaire philanthropist and father of one of their fallen comrades, had invited their former Navy SEAL team into a conference room at the end of the party and presented a proposal to be part of a private special task force company. River appreciated the opportunity—these were men he trusted, and he loved the money he could make to help fund his fight against human trafficking.

River asked Cannon and Zane to stay behind and give him some advice. Sutton already had a mission for him. Something in his gut didn't feel right, though. There just wasn't enough information, and it felt like a babysitting job.

Cannon and Zane both stared at him as he finished quietly sharing the few details he had about Sutton's request. "So it's perfect," River said, trying to convince himself as much as anyone.

"What's perfect about it?" Zane asked.

"I'll get a huge paycheck for an easy job, then I can plunge into the trafficking battle full-time, until Sutton has another job for me."

"But you have to go chasing off after the Duke of Gunthry's wild-child daughter, find her, and keep her safe for how long?" Cannon asked.

River's chair scraped back onto all four legs. Sutton had been really cryptic, and he wasn't the type of guy you begged for details. River was the soldier. Sutton was the general. Yet there'd been something in Sutton's eyes as he explained the mission—he cared deeply for someone involved in it. "We didn't get into a timeline."

"Just drag Alexandria Gunthry's beautiful body back to her daddy, you get the financial backing, and you're home free," Zane said.

"So there is a little problem, I guess," River admitted. "Sutton said I'm not supposed to bring her back home. I'm to watch over her on her 'adventure.' I assume her parents want her to sow her wild oats before she settles down and assumes her place in society."

"'In society'? What is this, eighteenth-century England?" Zane arched an eyebrow and flicked his thumb against the leg of his jeans. Some called him Thor because of his blond hair and the intimidating way he had, but River didn't always like the push back Zane put him through.

"When you're that wealthy, there are certain expectations. And yes, for them they probably are stuck in the social decrees of eighteenth-century England." River spoke from experience, and they both knew not to question him. He didn't really blame the girl for running away from the expectations, the dinners, the speaking engagements, the constant pressure to pretend you were perfect. Nobody wanted an errant hair out of place for the paparazzi to discuss. Alexandria had a lot more paparazzi following her than River had ever had to deal with. His father had "only" been a self-made billionaire with his worldwide importing business, and River had five other brothers to share the limelight with. *Her* family was royalty from England and quite possibly more wealthy than even his father. Plus she was perfectly beautiful, a single child, and had a wild streak a mile long. Paparazzi heaven.

River had been able to leave all the wealth and pomp behind at eighteen to join the Navy and work his way into becoming a SEAL. He'd formed a brotherhood with Cannon, Zane, Blayze, and Doug, Sutton's son, as well as with the rest of their team, and that bond extended beyond their early retirement. Sadly, Doug didn't make it back with them. Interesting that Sutton had decided to honor Doug's memory by forming a security team to work on special projects. In a lot of ways, River was relieved the word "team" was pretty loose. After all, Sutton had invited Corbin Spencer, and even though Corbin had been part of their platoon in SEAL Team 7, none of them trusted him to have their backs. The battle that had happened between Corbin and Zane at the meeting half an hour ago just reinforced that.

"I get the feeling you want to go find her," Cannon said.

He shrugged. Alexandria was intriguing to him, and not just because she had the face of an angel. He'd also escaped from his father like he assumed she was doing. Yet from what Sutton had said, her family was ultra-concerned about her, and the fact that Sutton hadn't instructed River to drag her back to England showed that her dad wasn't like River's dad. River's dad would've had somebody kick his butt and throw him on a plane back home. Luckily joining the Navy had been the perfect escape hatch. Even Daddy Warbucks couldn't buy his son back once he'd reached eighteen and committed himself. Now he only had to pretend he had a relationship with his father for certain social engagements. When he went home to visit, his dad was cordial but spent most of his time at the office, leaving River free to enjoy the company of his mom, brothers, two sisters-in-law, and four nephews.

"So Sutton already had a job lined up when he invited us all here tonight?" Zane pursed his lips. "Interesting."

"Maybe he and the duke know each other. Did you know Sutton was a commodore in the Royal Navy before he retired and relocated to America?"

Cannon arched an eyebrow. "But Doug was an American citizen?"

"Yeah."

"He's an interesting dude, that's for sure," Zane said.

River looked up. Sutton was slowly making his way their direction. He was tall with a handsome but craggy face and penetrating blue eyes. Though hints of gray were highlighting his well-kept beard and thick hair, it was obvious by the way he filled out his tux and the determination in his eyes that he was not somebody to mess with. He reminded River of Daniel Craig as James Bond.

"Time for a decision," Zane said.

"Do you have anything to lose?" Cannon asked.

"Good point." River would be glad having something to do, and the job didn't sound too hard—no deranged stalker or anything, just keep the girl from falling off a cliff or falling prey to one of the hippies camping along the Nā Pali coastline.

Zane stood. "All right. You go chase after Miss Debutante and we'll see what assignments come our way."

River grinned. "Well, boys, I'm off to Hawaii to find a beautiful woman."

"Sounds tough."

"It's a rough job, but somebody's got to do it."

Cannon inclined his chin toward him. "Heart of a warrior."

"Heart of a warrior," River and Zane repeated automatically, yet River always felt those words deeply and he was glad Sutton had chosen that phrase as their code that all was well. There was purpose to each mission. If only he knew what that purpose was in regards to Alexandria Gunthry.

———

Alexandria Gunthry pedaled her bike slowly along the path that ran from Lihue north to Kapa'a along the east side of the small island of Kauai. She inhaled the salty, humid air and grinned. She'd done it. Four days ago her mum had helped her escape from her father, their sprawling mansion in Kensington that was really more of a prison, and the arranged future marriage to Henry Poppleton that, at best, would choke the life and joy out of her.

Ally had broken away from her father and his heavy hand at eighteen financially and physically with the help of her mum and granddad. She'd only come back home to Kensington after graduating from Princeton with her master's because her granddad passed. Without Granddad around to keep her father in line, her mum was in more danger than ever.

All Ally wanted was to see her mum happy. Of course, her father didn't concern himself much with happiness, whether for her mum or for Ally herself. He faked kindness for a bit after she returned home, but Ally easily sensed the falseness of the duke's intentions. He planned to force her into marriage so he could make more money than he'd ever spend.

A union with Henry would assure her father's shipping company billions of pounds and more political clout for her father. The thought of marrying that puppet chilled Ally clear through. Henry was a weasel with lips like a codfish's, and Ally's intuition, which was always dead on, told her he was not only a wimp but a bully.

The only guilt she'd felt when escaping was leaving her mum, but of course Mum had not only encouraged her but helped her set it all up. She didn't want the life snuffed out of Ally. Mum was the first one to admit that she'd been exactly like Ally at her age, and look at her now. She held herself so regally, but her eyes were pools of neglect and abuse. Ally prayed that someday, somehow, her mum could escape. She'd begged her to come with her, but Mum insisted that the duke would make it a matter of national security if Mum came up missing. Elizabeth Gunthry, Duchess of Gunthry, was often touted as one of the most beautiful women in the world, and her job was to look good on the duke's arm. Ally, he could afford to be without, until her wedding day, at least. She shuddered. Maybe she'd get lucky and Henry would call it off, or she could stay hidden in Kauai until her father finally gave up. Not likely.

The beach trail ended and she rode along the side of the road. Traffic was consistent, but people drove slow and she felt perfectly safe. Nobody could rush on an island this beautiful. There were trees everywhere, many of them with orange, yellow, pink, or white flowers on them. Flowers on trees! She squealed happily. Slowing her speed, she kept her eyes peeled for the most brilliant spot along this road. The thick green mountainside parted and revealed a waterfall cascading down through the perfect greenery.

Ally stopped her bike and stared in awe as cars slowed and gawked along with her. A young girl rolled down her window and stuck her head out as her father slowed almost to a stop.

"I love it so much!" the little girl hollered.

"Me as well!" Ally shouted back.

The little girl gave Ally a thumbs-up. "It's almost as pretty as you!"

"Cheers!" Ally thanked her, agreeing the waterfall was beautiful and the little girl was adorable.

The family honked and waved at her before being forced to move on as traffic snuck up behind them.

Ally stared at the waterfall. This was one she couldn't swim in, but her research had revealed several that she could. She could hardly wait. Forcing herself to pedal away from the picturesque spot, she continued oohing and ahhing over the verdant mountain peaks and the crashing ocean expanse. She loved the warmth, the lush greenery, the laid-back pace, and the safe feel of Kauai.

Twenty minutes later, she coasted down the hill and over the one-lane bridge into Hanalai Bay. This valley was so overrun with greenery it looked like Vietnam to her.

Her stomach rumbled. Trip Advisor had given Chicken in a Barrel good marks and she wasn't one to argue with reviews. She locked up her bike and walked through the open-air shops, ducking into the restaurant and ordering barbecue chicken, ribs, chili, and coleslaw. She found a table up on the open balcony and sat, savoring the food and looking out at the forested mountains. The day was perfect for late February—high clouds, sunshine, green mountains, and blue seas greeted her. She'd been afraid all she'd see was rain this time of year, but so far there had only been brief afternoon showers that settled more like warm mist. Paradise, to be sure.

"This seat taken?" a nicely timbered voice asked.

Ally glanced up and took her time looking over him before she answered.

He arched an eyebrow and smiled. "Did I pass muster?"

"How do you do?"

He cocked his head to the side. "I'm good. You?"

Ally laughed. "I'm glad you're good, but 'how do you do' is more like 'hello.'"

"Hello." He smiled, and ooh, he was cute. "So I do pass muster?" He moved to sit down.

Ally held out a hand. "Not so quick, chump." His dark hair was short, military or missionary short, but it was nice—clean and thick and would probably feel good beneath her fingertips. His face was lean and proportioned with a firm jaw, a straight nose, and smooth, tanned skin. She liked the crinkles next to his eyes and mouth as he smiled at her, awaiting her perusal. He'd had some experiences in life, good and bad, if those crinkles told her anything. He was a big guy—broad and at least six-three with lots of lovely muscles peeking out from underneath his T-shirt and board shorts. It was his eyes that finally convinced her to accept his request. Their deep brown sparkled at her, though she could tell he could be very serious.

He tapped the edge of his tray. "How about now?"

"Okay, no harm in sharing a table." She grinned. "But I'm not keen on taking you home ... no matter how appealing those puppy-dog eyes are."

His eyebrows both went up at that. He set his tray down and slid into the seat. "Do you regularly take men home?"

"Don't get your hopes up." She winked at him and picked a bite of rib off the bone, savoring the tang of the barbecue sauce and the heartiness of the meat. No, she never took men home, only selectively dated those who passed her intuition test. She trusted her intuition completely and she could have fun with this hot, tough-looking guy.

He laughed and dug into his brisket. "Mm. This place is good."

"One of my favorites."

"Have you been on the island long?"

She wished. "A few days."

"Oh. You act like a local." He ate a bite of beans and took a drink of water before asking, "Which part of England are you from?"

"London. Kensington, to be exact. You?"

"Long Island originally. I like your accent a lot."

"I've been in the States for over six years, so it's faded."

"Don't let it fade."

That made her smile. "So, I'm Ally."

He nodded. "Pleasure to meet you."

"And you are?" He didn't seem to reveal much, but he was super attractive and was putting off good vibes. She prided herself on being able to read people, and this good-looking man had a great aura—confident and strong but mindful of others. Ally had no problem making a new friend.

"River."

"And what are your plans today, River?"

"Besides eating lunch with you?"

She smiled. "Yeah, besides that."

"I was hoping to go on a hike. You know any good ones?"

"For sure. Fancy a buddy?" She took a bite of the chunky chili.

"I'd love one."

"Let's do it." She took a long sip of water and appraised him. This day kept getting better and better. Picturesque scenery, beautiful weather, nice bike ride, yummy lunch, and now a fine-looking buddy to go on a hike with.

They finished lunch and walked toward the parking lot. "I need to run by my house to pick up my trainers and backpack," Ally said. "Do you want to meet up in half an hour?"

"Sure. Where?"

She gave him directions to the Nā Pali coastline hike trailhead and walked away. Turning back, she saw him watching and gave him a little wave. Yep, he was cute, yet he had a little bit of a bad-boy feel. She grinned to herself. Running away from home was definitely the best move she'd made.

CHAPTER TWO

RIVER WATCHED Alexandria walk to her bike with his fists clenched and disbelief filling his head. She had no clue who he was and she'd checked him out, flirted with him, and then eagerly agreed to go on a hike. Was she completely innocent, stupid, not caring who she hooked up with, or a little of all of the above? He'd assumed the daughter of a duke would be stuffy and proper and a pretty easy person to follow around and keep safe. True, she had a reputation for being a fun, free spirit, but not for sleeping around. Hopefully the reports were right. If he had to watch her flit through man after man, he might intervene and get himself fired.

Ally was friendly, beautiful, and much too trusting. What a nightmare.

He drove to the home Sutton had set up for him, across the street from Ally's rented house on Hanalei Bay. He saw her lock her bike up and ducked so she wouldn't see him. Soon enough he'd have to tell her who he was, but he wanted a little more time to observe and see what would be expected of him on this job. If she acted around all men like she'd been with him a few minutes ago, he would definitely need round-the-clock surveillance. Thankfully he'd brought the cameras for that.

He changed into hiking shoes and threw some water bottles and granola bars into a small backpack, then drove to the trailhead. It was almost three, so they only had a few hours of daylight left. He wondered if she had enough sense to even realize that. She seemed like a fly-by-the-seat-of-her-pants kind of girl. In another world, she'd be interesting to him. In his security world ... no way.

River was standing by the trailhead watching for her when Ally pulled into the parking lot in a white rental Jeep, a twin to his own rental. She found an open stall in the busy parking lot and bee-bopped out of her Jeep. Dressed in a tank top and yoga capris, she pranced over to where he waited. "Hey, there. You up for it?"

"Sure."

"Let's do this."

She strode past him with a grin and started climbing the dirt-packed trail. Luckily it hadn't rained for a few days, so it wasn't as muddy as he'd heard it usually was. He followed behind her and he couldn't pretend he didn't like the view, but his mind was spinning trying to figure out how to keep her safe without her realizing who he was. Sutton hadn't cared if he revealed himself or not, as long as he kept her safe for her family, but this afternoon was about feeling out the assignment.

A lot of hikers were coming the other direction, but nobody was headed toward Hanakapi'ai Beach, or the farther hike to the water-fall, this late in the day. Ally set a great pace, and even though he'd kept in top shape after leaving the military, he wouldn't call this an easy hike and he'd eaten a bit too much at lunch. His stomach was churning as they crested the rise and hit the mile mark. The view was incredible of the leafy green mountainside and the beach and ocean far below. They cruised down the other side, greeting all the hikers headed out, and finally reached the two-mile point and the beach covered with boulders.

Ally stopped and whirled to face him. She pulled a water bottle out of her backpack and took a long drink. River followed suit. Sweat was dripping down his back. The humidity was definitely higher than San Diego.

"You up for hiking to the waterfall?" she asked.

He lifted an eyebrow. "Will we make it back out before dark?"

"Blimey! It's only two miles. We'll make out fine if you stop slowing me down."

River wanted to respond, but her accent had him in some sort of trance, so he laughed and gestured to the trail. "Lead the way."

The next couple of miles got more intense. They had to climb over boulders and either wade through the river or shimmy from rock to rock. River had seen a lot of gorgeous terrain when he'd been stationed in the Philippines, but Kauai's lush mountains, rivers, waterfalls, and beaches could hold their own with any scenery.

They finally reached the end of the trail and the waterfall, both pausing on the boulders to stare up in awe. A decent stream of water cascaded down hundreds of feet over mossy green rock and ended in a wide pool. The water in the pool wasn't clear enough to see the bottom, but it flowed down the river they'd hiked next to and wasn't stagnant.

The pool and surrounding rocks were deserted as the sun was low in the sky. River looked around and his stomach dropped. How dare Ally come to some isolated paradise with a man she didn't know? She'd checked him out and seen how well-built he was. It made him sick to his stomach that she was so clueless. Anyone could take advantage of her.

As they reached the pebbled area next to the waterfall, she gave him a mischievous glance and then dropped her backpack, turned, and ran straight into the pool. Diving into the water, she swam toward the waterfall. The force of the water drove her back away from it, splashing water into her face.

River stared. This girl was nuts. He would think she was fun if he wasn't responsible for her safety.

"Come on, chum," Ally hollered to him.

River blew out a breath, dropped his backpack, and peeled off his shirt. No reason to be completely wet when he got out.

Ally's eyes swept over his chest as he walked toward her and she gave him a coy grin. This girl was trouble. No wonder her parents had been so willing to pay top dollar for River to protect her. Hopefully it was simply protecting her from herself. If there was a stalker or someone bent on hurting her, this innocent creature would be done for.

He stepped into the water and shivered. You'd think all water in Hawaii was warm, but it was February and the source was coming out of a mountain. Bracing himself, he dove in and swam quickly to Ally. The spray from the falls was strong. It stung his face, but he'd been born to be in the water and it didn't bother him.

"Isn't this the bee's knees?" she asked, all childlike exuberance.

"Yeah."

They treaded water next to the downpour from the waterfall for maybe half a minute; then she grinned and splashed some water at him before swimming away. She stopped and stood in water about waist deep. Water streamed down her smooth, tanned skin and her wet hair looked like gold. Her tank top clung to her chest and abdomen. She was far too beautiful and apparently clueless of that fact.

In a dozen strokes River was next to her and stood on the uneven boulders that made up the bottom of the pool.

She glanced up at the greenery surrounding them and the water cascading down. "It's so ... invigorating."

She stuttered a step and River moved forward to steady her. The rocks were slippery and unstable. "You okay?"

"Yes. Thanks for sharing this with me! Cheers!" She threw her arms around his neck and planted a kiss on his lips. Her lithe body was warm against his chest and her lips were soft and seemed to mold perfectly to his. She pulled back, laughed, and dove under the water like some sea nymph.

River sat there, stunned. That kiss had been sweet and innocent yet warmed him all the way to his bones. She couldn't really act like this with every guy she'd met; she wouldn't have any of the innocence left that leapt from her bright blue eyes. Didn't she realize how dangerous this was? Being alone with some guy she didn't know was one thing, but flinging herself at him and kissing him? So many men would take advantage of her quicker than she could blink.

Now where was she? He glanced around the small pool. Had the waterfall gotten a hold of her and pummeled her against the rocks?

He was coiling to dive in after her when she surfaced and wiped the water off of her face. "Isn't this fun?"

River couldn't take it any longer. He pushed through the water, grabbed her arm, and hauled her back onto dry ground.

"Are you daft?" she asked, her eyes finally wide with fear. Maybe there was an ounce of sense in that pretty head. "Let me go!"

River released her arm, but he stayed right in her face. "Are *you* completely insane?"

She blinked up at him. "Because I swam in a waterfall?"

"No." He ground his teeth. "Some guy picks you up at lunch and you invite him to go hiking to an isolated spot?"

She backed up a step. "I don't think it's usually this ... quiet."

"Well, it's quiet right now," he thundered, making up the step she'd taken. He wrapped his hands around her arms, ignoring the warm rush he felt at touching her. Her eyes darted down to his hands, then back up to meet his. "And then you kissed me?" He shook his head. "You are completely and maddeningly naïve. Do you realize how many men would take advantage of you right now?"

Ally let out a small squeak and looked up at him, her blue eyes concerned yet still filled with trust and hope. "But you wouldn't."

River could *not* believe her. "You think you're some judge of character?" he asked. "How do you know what I would or wouldn't do to you?" He felt bad that he was scaring her, but she needed a good scare. She needed to be terrified and stay in safe places and—

best-case scenario—head back to her family. Her father should've demanded River bring her back home immediately and locked her away somewhere safe. Oh, she was making his head hurt.

"Kindly let me go," she whispered, her blue eyes uncertain and finally wary.

River released her.

She scurried away from him and grabbed her backpack. "Shall we head back down, then?" Without awaiting his answer, she flipped her backpack on and started down the trail, water streaming from her hair and clothes.

River let out a groan, grabbed his T-shirt, pulled it on, put his backpack on, and followed her. This was his worst nightmare. Maybe he should see if Zane would trade him assignments. Surely whatever job Sutton had delegated to him would be better than this. Yet the thought of Zane being kissed by Ally made his stomach churn. He'd stay here and protect her, but he knew he wasn't going to be happy about it.

CHAPTER THREE

ALLY'S HEAD was pounding with fear and regret as she half-ran down the uneven, boulder-strewn trail. River stayed close behind her and his words rushed through her head over and over again. *You are completely and maddeningly naïve. Do you realize how many men would take advantage of you right now?* Her granddad used to tell her she was too trusting. She knew it was an issue, but she *could* read people. She always knew who had nefarious intent and who didn't. She'd sensed right from the start that River was a warrior, but he had a good heart. Had her intuition failed her?

The sun set behind the mountain and her fear ratcheted up a few notches. They reached the beach that meant they had two miles left. It was completely deserted.

"Do you understand why you should be concerned?" River said too close to her ear.

Ally jumped and stumbled through the uneven rocks in the river toward the trail back to the parking lot. She was wet, miserable, and scared. Two more miles and she could lock herself in her Jeep, race to her rental home, and pray she never saw him again. Then again, why would he say what he did, basically announce he planned to take advantage of her, if he really did intend to do that? He could've easily done something back at the waterfall.

No. He was a faker and she was safe. She kept repeating that over and over again in her head. *Please let me be safe.*

Oh, her mum would be devastated if she got raped and killed. Ally straightened her spine as she marched up the dirt-packed trail. She was stronger and braver than even her mum knew. That was why she'd come to this exotic escape, because she was never going to let a man have power over her again, like her mum had dealt with her entire life. Luckily she had her mum helping her and silently cheering her on, and money wasn't an issue. Her granddad had transferred most of his fortune—several billion pounds—into a trust fund solely in Ally's name the day Ally turned eighteen. Her undergrad at Princeton had been in finance, and with a little knowledge she'd proven to be amazing at playing the stock market and choosing companies to do hard money loans and start-up funds for. Her intuition again. How had it failed her today?

It felt like River was breathing down her neck as they ascended the top of the trail and started back down the other side. She hurried faster as the sky darkened. Her trainers were packed with mud from getting them wet in the waterfall and the river and then walking on the dirty, sometimes muddy trail. She skidded down a steep part where a spring must've been running from above. River put out a hand to steady her.

Ally pulled away quickly. She'd felt all kinds of brilliant sparks before he'd turned mad-scary at the waterfall after she kissed him. She liked him touching her way too much, and that meant that her intuition was definitely on the fritz. How could she have messed up this bad?

She picked up the pace and jogged down the hill, sliding a little bit in spots, but they'd get there before dark, hopefully. It was getting harder and harder to see where she was placing her steps, and the drop to her left was a little disconcerting.

Her right foot came down on a large slick rock and slipped out from under her. She heard and felt the ligaments in her ankle snap. "Oh!" she gasped, limping to a stop.

River stopped behind her. "What happened?"

"Blimey, I just ... twisted my bloomin' ankle."

"Can you walk on it?"

"Yes," she barked out. She was normally happy and upbeat, but this whole day had been ruined by River. She didn't like questioning her own judgment and being afraid. Yet she was more and more certain that River was a bluffer. If he would've wanted to hurt her, wouldn't he have done it already?

She took a step. Pain shot through her ankle, and she winced. "Aw, no."

River wrapped his arm around her waist. "Put your weight on me."

That didn't help at all. When her breath should've been short from fear, it was short from something else entirely. Her heart rate shot through the roof and all she could think about was the feel of his brawny arm around her and his hand cupping her hip. She'd dated her fair share of fun and good-looking American men spending six years in New Jersey, but she'd never seen the likes of him. She kept shuffling down the hillside and ignored the impression of warmth and safety. River was a good guy, even if he obviously wanted to terrify her. Maybe he had a lot of sisters and was just trying to help her be more aware. Or maybe he was a psychopath who toyed with his victims before he raped and killed them. *Oh, stop, imagination.*

They progressed a little way down the trail as the darkness deepened around them.

"This isn't working," River said. He swooped her legs out from under her and lifted her into the air like she weighed nothing.

"Stop!" Ally's heartbeat thundered in her ears as she instinctively grabbed his muscular shoulders for stability. "What are you doing?"

"We've got to get you down this mountain before we have to camp out here for the night."

The thought of being alone with him all night both thrilled and terrified her. What was wrong with her? He was moving quickly down the trail and there was enough light left to see the huge drop-off to their left. Ally didn't mind heights, but she liked being on her own two feet. She held on to his shoulders a little tighter.

"You'd probably like that, wouldn't you?" he asked.

"What?" She glanced up at his chiseled jawline. She would've liked him if he wasn't so abrupt and scary.

"Spending the night with me."

Ally pulled her arms from around his shoulders and slapped him right across the cheek. He blinked at her but didn't even flinch as he kept carrying her down the steep trail.

"I don't get off with anyone," she flung at him.

"I'm glad to hear you have a little bit of sense."

"Argh! Why are you being such a git to me? I thought you were nice when I first met you."

"Never believe first impressions."

"This is the first time my intuition has been wrong," she insisted.

"I'm sure there'll be a second."

Ally folded her arms across her chest, bouncing as he stepped over rocks and stayed close to the mountain and away from the cliff to their left. "I think you're a nutter," she spat at him.

"What?" It was getting harder and harder to see anything, but she was close enough to read the mocking tilt of his eyebrow and the way he seemed to be hiding laughter with his cheek twitching.

"First of all, my intuition has never been wrong. Second, if you were going to hurt me, you would've done it up at the waterfall when we were all alone."

He stopped and looked down at her for a few seconds that seemed to stretch into eternity. His brown eyes were warm and he studied her like he was trying to fit her into a box. He shifted her in his arms, lifting her a bit higher and tighter to his body. "Can you please put your arms around my neck so it's easier to carry you?"

It was Ally's turn to smirk. She kept her arms right where they were. "No, thank you. I didn't ask you to carry me."

"Just when I start to think you might not be the spoiled brat everyone claims you to be, you prove me wrong yet again."

"Oh!" She gasped out. So he'd known who she was all along? For some reason, that hurt. He wasn't interested in Ally; he was interested in the famous persona she portrayed. "You know nothing about me but what the media suggests."

"I'm a much better judge of character than you are." He grinned at her.

Ally's jaw dropped.

River started walking down the incline again, but he was moving much slower, picking his way along. It was so dark she wondered how he could see anything, especially with her in his arms obstructing his vision.

Tentatively, she wrapped her fingers around her ankle, and was relieved to find that the pain had diminished. "I can walk," she said. When he didn't answer, she told him, "Put me down. You can't see anything holding me."

"I can see you, and that's enough." He grinned at her and his cheek crinkled. He could probably be irresistible if he wanted to be, but she wasn't going to play his games.

"Please," she tried again.

River stopped and simply stared at her. His eyes dipped to her lips, then came up to meet hers again. It was much too intimate with him holding her close to his chest, and their faces were so close she could feel his warm breath on her cheek. She was uncomfortable with his perusal, yet warm all over from the look in his eyes and the strength in his arms.

Without a word, he released her legs and let her feet slide to the ground. Ally winced as she put pressure on her ankle, but it wasn't bad. She was pretty sure she could walk it off. River's other arm was still around her back and he kept her by his side as he continued to stare at her. She tried to start forward, but he held her in place.

"Let's go," she insisted.

"Like I told you earlier. You shouldn't assume I don't have evil intent."

She stared up at him, barely able to make out his features in the dark. Her heart thumped hard and fast. "Why do you keep trying to scare me?" she whispered.

"Because I want you to open your eyes." His voice softened. "And I don't want to see you get hurt."

She swallowed and looked down. At least he wasn't going to hurt her. He was a warrior clear through, and it seemed as if he wanted to protect her. "I'll try to be more careful."

"Thank you." He kept his arm tight around her waist and they shuffled down the last half mile to the parking lot.

When they reached her Jeep, he let her go. She felt cold and alone without his arm holding her up. She fished her keys out of her backpack, clicked the unlock button, and jerked the door open. He stood within reaching distance, but he felt terribly far away. What did she care? She didn't even know him and she was done with men controlling her life. She'd finally escaped from her dad and Henry; there was no reason to replace them with another male, no matter how attractive he was.

"Is your ankle all right?" he asked.

Ally nodded quickly. "Yes. Thank you for your help."

"Anytime." He gave her a brief smile, then stepped back.

She climbed into her Jeep and tossed her backpack on the passenger seat. The vehicle was already filthy with mud and sand from all the hiking and beach time she'd had the past few days.

Starting the vehicle and pulling it into gear, she could only see River's shadow as she pulled away. Was it possible to be attracted to someone yet apprehensive about them at the same time? She'd never thought she was one to fall for the bad boy, but River fit the description of bad-boy-slash-hot-honey like no one she'd ever met. She shivered, anxious to be showered and safe in her rental home. Would she see River again? At this point she didn't know what to hope for.

CHAPTER FOUR

RIVER SHOWERED and fell asleep shortly after he got home. He naturally woke up at four a.m., since it would've been six at home. After doing a few rounds of push-ups, planks, pull-ups, and jump squats, he showered and ate a quick breakfast. Packing a bag with water and some snack food, he loaded into his white Jeep. He sat in the driveway of his rental house, where he could see when Ally left. He needed to set up some surveillance equipment tonight so he didn't have to sit and wait as much or possibly miss her. It was a miracle she'd survived life this long unscathed. This woman needed him.

Half an hour later, while the sky was still bluish-black, Ally's garage door went up and she backed out. He wondered if her ankle would keep her from exploring today. Maybe he'd get lucky and she'd just go sit on a beach somewhere. But then she wouldn't be leaving at six-thirty in the morning to sit somewhere. Kauai's beaches were not that crowded.

He sank down in his seat as her lights flashed over his Jeep. She drove past and he waited for a ten count before starting his vehicle and flipping it around. He made a mental note to also put a tracker on her Jeep. It was going to be hard to follow her in the early morning when they were probably the only two people on the road.

He followed her for about half an hour around the west side of the island to Kapa'a, where she turned right onto a side road. The sun rose as she drove through beautiful scenery and established neighborhoods. It seemed more like a spot that locals would live with a variety of more- and less-expensive homes. When she pulled off the road and stopped at a trailhead parking lot, he kept driving. He went around the next couple of curves, waited five minutes, then doubled back. There was only one other car in the parking lot. He parked as far away from her Jeep as he could, but it was a pretty small parking lot.

Grabbing his backpack, he started up the trail. The incline was decent but not anything too strenuous. He could've run up it, but he didn't want to catch up to her and risk being seen. There were so many switchbacks and places to stop and admire the view he quit counting. On one he saw her long, blonde ponytail. She was setting a good pace; apparently the ankle was feeling better.

Between the morning sun coming out full force and the strenuous hike, he had sweat dripping down his back. At least he would be getting plenty of exercise in with this assignment. How long could he keep following her without her knowing it? Maybe he shouldn't have introduced himself to get to know her a little bit yesterday. It might make tracking her more difficult, but he'd done it to learn if she was smart about her protection or not. He'd gotten plenty of insight and realized she was completely clueless about being safe and men in general. Shaking his head, he still couldn't believe she'd kissed him at the waterfall. Even worse was the way his body had reacted. He had better self-control than to get all bothered by any beautiful woman that touched him, but the feel of her in his arms as he carried her down the trail wasn't leaving his memory either.

He walked along a ridge, noticing he was at the highest point of the mountain. She'd probably be turning around soon. To his shock, he realized she was standing on a rocky ledge about a hundred feet away from him. Her arms were out wide like she was embracing the whole world. He was no wuss about heights, but he hated the way she was standing on the edge of the cliff, with nothing below her but a quick death. He admired people who were fearless, but there was a point of sheer stupidity and she was flirting with that line.

Her eyes were focused out over the valley. She brought her hands to her heart, raised one foot, and tucked it into her other thigh. He cursed. What was she doing? Yoga on the point. Was she shooting some idiotic YouTube video?

River clenched and unclenched his fists, staring at her. She was beautiful, no doubt, but he liked the women he dated to have a brain in their heads. He shook his own head. What was he thinking? The kiss meant nothing and he was on a job. His first job for Sutton would be his last if he didn't stop fantasizing about his protection detail.

Ally gracefully switched legs and brought her hands up above her head. River was about ready to run the rest of the way up the trail and drag her away from that ledge when she put her leg down and stepped back. He released a pent-up breath. He'd seen enough death with the SEALs. The thought of this beautiful woman's broken body on the rocks far below sent a shudder through him.

Maybe it was time he revealed who he was and demanded she let him stay close. But what if she balked at that? Sutton had said she was fleeing from her responsibilities at home. Knowing that her family had sent someone after her might make her do something even crazier than yoga on the edge of a cliff.

River turned and started back down the trail, saying hello to a young couple coming up a switchback. He wanted to make it to his Jeep before her so he could hide out and be able to follow her wherever she was going next. Yes, a tracker on her vehicle would definitely lessen his stress. He'd have to remember to grab one out of his equipment bag at home and find a way to put it on next time she went off on an adventure. With this girl the adventure might be nonstop.

Footsteps pounded a ways behind him. River swiveled to see who was coming, and sure enough, he glimpsed her blonde hair. He looked around for a place to hide, but there was nothing. Sprinting down the trail, he leapt over exposed roots and scrambled over boulders. His heart was thundering in his ears and he hated the position he was in. One wrong move and he'd roll down part of the trail or plunge off a cliff, but he had to get to the parking lot first or she might disappear on him.

He passed hikers as he went, offering a quick greeting but not slowing down. A few muttered their frustration when he brushed past them. He flew down the last switchback and flung himself into his Jeep. Seconds later, she appeared. He felt bad for wishing her ankle injury would've been worse.

She tossed her backpack into the back seat, climbed in, and drove off. Luckily there were a lot more vehicles in the parking lot now and she hadn't seemed to notice River. Had she seen him on the trail?

He followed her down to Kapa'a and then up a different side road. This time he could read the sign: Wailua Falls. She drove quickly and he kept pace. When she pulled into the small parking lot he thought he'd keep driving nonchalantly, but the road dead-ended at the parking lot. He found a spot three up from her and slouched down in his seat, waiting. There were warning signs all over not to hike down to the falls, so she was probably just going to look at the view.

He saw her get out of her vehicle and talk to the homeless guy making baskets out of leaves and protecting his pig. Then she walked back down the road fifty feet to a chain-link fence and climbed over the cement block next to it. What in the world was she doing now? She disappeared from his view and he grabbed his keys and backpack and hurried out of his Jeep. This woman was insane. He approached the homeless guy.

"Aloha," the guy greeted him.

"The blonde girl you were just talking to—where is she going?"

The guy patiently stared at him.

"Please. I'm supposed to be protecting her. The warning signs say it's not safe to go down to the waterfall."

The man nodded, then said, "The young ones all want to swim in the falls."

"So she went down there?"

The man nodded again.

With a curse, River ran toward where Ally had disappeared. "Maholo!" he called over his shoulder. The guy raised a hand.

River vaulted over the concrete block and almost launched himself off a cliff. "Whoa!" He grabbed onto the chain-link fence, his heart racing. Easing himself along the edge, he searched for a way down. He finally saw a muddy spot that looked like it was at least passable, so he scurried down the incline, clinging to roots and vines whenever possible, sliding on his butt sometimes in his efforts not to plunge to his death. He couldn't see Ally anywhere. If he ran into her, what would he say? He gritted his teeth. He'd tell her to stop being so stupid. Maybe shake some sense into that beautiful head. The girl either had a death wish or was completely clueless.

He got to a more manageable part of the trail and ran into some teenagers who were coming up. The skinny one with a mop of curly brown hair grinned at him, "Hey, dude, did you seriously come down that?" He pointed to the steep incline.

"Yeah."

The taller, blond kid laughed and pointed to their left. "That's the trail. It's a lot easier."

"Thanks." He pushed out a breath, calming himself. "I'll try that next time."

They both took off, laughing. River couldn't help but chuckle. He'd taken the wrong route down. Maybe Ally wasn't quite as crazy as he was giving her credit for. With a huff, he hurried down the rest of the trail. Some parts had ropes to assist him, and it wasn't nearly as bad as what he'd done at the first.

At last he reached some lava rock and the pool at the bottom of the waterfall opened up to him. On the far side of the rocks stood Ally. She'd stripped off her tank top and shorts, revealing a crop top sort of suit with tight shorts-like bottoms. He had no clue about swimsuit styles, but he really liked this one that revealed her lean arms and legs and a smooth hint of her abdomen. She climbed into the pool, then took off swimming for the other side. The waterfall was so strong that it sent waves rippling outwards. Ally appeared to be a strong swimmer, but he was going to watch her close, all the while wishing he could be in the water with her.

One thing he could say about this girl: she definitely wasn't a spectator in life.

———

Ally had loved her hike early this morning to the crest of the Sleeping Giant, but it felt even better to swim in the pool at the bottom of the fabulous Wailua waterfall. Basking in Kauai's beauty, she could almost forget about Henry trying to force her into marriage, how beaten down her mum was, and how she knew this reprieve would only last until her father somehow found her. The duke always did. Her mum wouldn't rat her out, but her father was a scheming prat. He wore a politician's charming smile to the world, but believed his wife and daughter were only created to further his ambitions. Somehow, someway, her father would force her to marry Henry. She knew it, and horror churned in her gut. Henry would make her more miserable than her mum was, if that was possible.

Forcing it all from her thoughts, Ally turned over and floated on her back. The waves and the spray from the waterfall splashed over her face, but she didn't mind. She loved the water and as a child had prayed nonstop to turn into a mermaid and escape far from her father's manipulations and silky, lying tongue. The only thing that had kept her sane was her mum. Now her prayers had changed. She prayed her mum would get strong enough to escape her father and that Ally would somehow find a way to avoid her arranged marriage with Henry, forever.

She flipped upright and treaded water, now on the far side of the falls. As she looked across the pool, she noticed a couple of men swimming down by where the river continued, and beyond them a man was hanging back, watching. Watching her. Her eyes narrowed as she tried to make out his features. He turned away quickly and disappeared back up the trail. All she could tell was he was muscular and tall and it felt like he'd been watching her.

A chill ran down her backbone, but she shook it off. Lots of men watched her. At home it was because she was well-known, but she also knew that she was beautiful and men liked to check her out. It was no big deal, and her mum had always taught her that she was so much more than her lovely face and fit body.

She swam back across the pool, the waves splashing her face. The water was dirty, lots of natural, floating debris coming off the waterfall, but she loved it. Reluctantly, she pulled herself onto the rocks. Two fun adventures today. Too bad she had nobody to share this gorgeous island with, but she wouldn't have dared bring any of her college friends with her. They were great but hooked on social media. One errant picture of her posted to Instagram and her father would find her and haul her bum home faster than she could blink. She'd understood a little about American freedoms in her six years at Princeton under her granddad's protection, but her father's power seemed to encompass the entire Earth. She shivered, grateful for the warm breeze.

Ally tugged her clothes back on over her wet Nani swimsuit. She sloshed back up the trail and to her Jeep, only getting her trainers a little bit more muddy. She should've packed her Keens. As she climbed into her Jeep, she glanced up the parking lot and saw a white Jeep just like hers with a man sitting in it. She couldn't see the man clearly, but the Jeep looked exactly like the one she'd seen at the Sleeping Giant trailhead, and she could've sworn a Jeep like that followed her from the north side of the island early this morning.

She rolled her eyes at herself. Pretty much every rental on this island was white and a Jeep or something similar. She was being too paranoid. Her father couldn't have found her this quickly. She and her mum had worked it all out. She'd used a counterfeit name on a credit card and passport for the flight, rental home, and rental car, and was using cash for everything else. She was safe.

As she drove down the picturesque mountain road and turned back north onto the main road, she wished she could take the top off the Jeep. There was only the one main road that went around the island, so traffic was slow, but Ally rolled down her window and enjoyed the slower pace of the island. The rental company had told her that it rained too often to have the top off, especially where she was staying on the rainy side on the north.

She stopped at a food van for lunch in Kapa'a, grabbed a fish taco and a POG, and then asked Siri to direct her to Hideaway Beach. Twenty minutes later she pulled into a small parking lot by a tennis court. She hopped out of her Jeep and headed to the trail, ready to eat, play in the ocean, then just relax and bask in the sun. The locals kept telling her she was lucky that it had only rained intermittently, and she was thrilled. Only the sun could chase the darkness of England and her father away.

———

River followed Ally's Jeep to a small parking lot, which of course was full. He parked illegally in a condo parking lot and followed her to yet another trailhead. The ocean wasn't too far away but looked to be a decent drop. Was he in for another adventure course? As he reached the descent with ropes and PVC pipe to hold on to, he smiled. It didn't appear that Ally went for the easy way, ever. One of the SEALs' sayings was, *The only easy day was yesterday*. Ally seemed

like she'd appreciate that saying. There were dozens of easily acces-
sible and beautiful beaches on this small island, but no, she went for
the hidden beach with a muddy, jungle-gym type of trail. If he
weren't assigned to keep her safe, he'd like this girl a lot.

He climbed to the overlook above the beach and sucked in a
breath. This beach was definitely worth the rough terrain to get
here. The water was aqua blue, looking more like the Caribbean
than Hawaii. Gentle waves rolled into the light-brown sand, and as
he watched, a small turtle popped his head up for a breath. He
wished he had some scuba or at least snorkel gear. That water was
so clear he might not need any gear to see the wonders below.

His eyes scanned the small beach and his stomach dropped
when he realized there were only two people on it besides Ally. He
couldn't possibly go down there without blowing his cover. Ally had
spread out a towel and was slipping out of her shoes as he watched.
Forcing himself to look away as she slid out of her tank top and
shorts, he looked around and made sure there were no other ways
for her to leave except for this trail. Though every part of his body
wanted to go down to that soft-looking sand and explore the ocean
with his beautiful assignment, he forced himself to turn around and
trudge back up to his Jeep. He'd find a good spot to watch for her
to leave. He was hungry and irritable. He never liked being denied
an opportunity to play in the ocean. Surveillance bit the big one
sometimes.

CHAPTER FIVE

ALLY ABSOLUTELY FANCIED HIDEAWAY BEACH, and after eating her delicious fish tacos, she snorkeled and saw all kinds of fish and six adorable turtles. Then she stretched out on her towel in the soft sand and slept for a while in the warm sun. The sun set behind the hillside much too early for her liking. She drove back to her rental house, showered, and went to dinner at Kalypso. Her fresh-catch pesto pasta was incredible and the waiter was fun and seemed to enjoy chatting her up and giving her tips on what she couldn't miss on the island.

Still, she hated to admit how lonely it was eating by herself. Not lonely enough to want to go home and give in to her father's demands, but lonely enough she missed her mum and all her college friends. If she texted them she knew one of them would take a holiday and come experience this beautiful island with her, but she just didn't dare. What she really wished was that her mum would've been brave enough to escape her father's tentacles and come with her, but she knew that would never happen, especially with her granddad gone and most of the world believing her father to be some upstanding model citizen, her mum to be an empty-headed beauty, and Ally to be a wild child.

She strolled back to her lovely rental house, opened some windows so she could hear the waves crash, and started reading a Texas Titan Romance on her Kindle. The waves sounded luscious, but they were often drowned out by the obnoxious roosters so prevalent on this island. Even at the top of Sleeping Giant this morning, she could hear them. She tuned it out and enjoyed her book.

Around ten, she forced herself to go upstairs to bed, knowing she'd be up early with the time change. Lying there, all she could hear were the stupid roosters. She got up and made sure every window was closed, took some melatonin, and lay back down. Squeezing her eyes shut, she hoped she could sleep, but the nonstop crowing was driving her nuts. There had to be a stupid rooster squatting below the long patio that stretched the length of the master suite.

"Argh!" she screamed, throwing back the covers. "I am finding that rooster and I'm going to shut him up." She had no clue how—she'd never done anything violent to an animal in her life—but she couldn't lie there any longer.

———

River climbed down from a banyan tree outside Ally's rental house. She'd finally turned her lights out and gone to sleep half an hour ago. He'd almost gotten all the cameras placed in unnoticeable spots. He debated breaking into her garage and putting the tracker on her Jeep so he could keep up with her on her treks tomorrow, but maybe he should wait. The camera's sensors would alert him when she started moving in the morning and he could probably place the tracker on her Jeep at the first spot she stopped.

He'd stepped around the tree when he heard someone calling,

"Here, rooster, rooster. Come here so I can wring your neck, little rooster."

Was it Ally? It sounded like her voice.

What on earth? River eased around the edge of the house, and a body hurled toward him, then slammed into his shoulder. He grabbed the woman around the waist to steady her, and froze. It was Ally.

It was a dark night with only a sliver of a moon, but his eyes had adjusted enough to see the shock on her face. She tried to pull back, but he had a tight grip on her. She let out a cute little squeak.

River realized she was terrified. "Ally, it's okay, it's me, River." He felt like he knew her so well, but then he remembered she only knew him as the jerk who'd scared her after she'd impulsively kissed him. With her so close, he couldn't think of anything but that kiss.

"What are you doing here?" she demanded.

He released her and ran a hand through his short hair. "I was just out for ... a walk, and I heard you yelling at the rooster."

Her eyes filled with suspicion.

"My rental house is right there." He pointed across the street and was glad that he was telling the truth right now. She'd told him that she had intuition about things and it seemed like she could sense that he wasn't out for a walk.

"Interesting." She folded her arms across her chest and narrowed her eyes at him. Then, suddenly, she asked, "Are the roosters keeping you up all blasted night as well?"

River's eyebrows lifted at her abrupt change. Either she didn't want to know if he was stalking her, or she really was the most innocent and trusting female he'd ever met. "I can sleep through most anything." SEAL training had taught him to sleep when he could, but he could wake at any time also, which he was counting on in the morning when his sensors went off and he had to chase after her on whatever adventures she was planning for tomorrow.

Her eyes traveled over him. "Let me guess: you did some kind of elite special warrior training where you learned to sleep in extreme and uncomfortable conditions."

River swayed but didn't step back like instinct was telling him to.

She put a hand on his arm. "So that means ..."

River couldn't imagine she was okay with him being paid to watch out for her, but if she'd guessed the truth she was acting great about it. Had his job just gotten much easier?

"You can kill the manky rooster for me."

River couldn't hold in his laughter. "I didn't figure you for the violent type."

"Even after I slapped you?" She put her hand over her mouth.

River shook his head. He had forgotten about that. "How's your ankle?"

"Fine. I walked it out this morning."

He'd followed her on that "walk." She was intense.

"You want to come in for some tea to help me sleep?"

River's eyes widened. How in the world was she this naïve?

"Oh ... stop, I'm bonkers. You'll tell me that I should never invite a strange man into my house, correct? Forget I asked."

He had no clue how to respond to her and wondered how she'd survived before he was assigned to watch over her. "How old are you?" he demanded.

"Twenty-four. How old are you?"

What did it matter how old he was? He'd only asked her because he couldn't believe she was over sixteen and this innocent. "Twenty-eight," he finally said.

"Nice. The perfect spread of ages."

River licked his lips. She was flirting with him. If he hadn't been assigned to watch over her, this conversation would be going in a completely different direction, but he held back the comments he wanted to make.

When he didn't respond, she glanced away at the chickens and roosters wandering around, highlighted by a streetlight. "So ... are you going to throttle my rooster with your bare hands?"

Several of the birds started their cockle-doodle-doo again as River tried not to laugh. She was cute. "Um, Ally?"

"Yes?"

"If you haven't noticed, there are more roosters on this island than humans. Even if you disposed of twenty, you'd still hear them all night long."

Her shoulders drooped. "So your advice is ..."

"Ear plugs?"

She smiled. "Okay. I'll pick some up in the morning." She backed up a step. "Maybe I'll see you around."

"It's a small island." He grinned back at her. Maybe this job wouldn't be as hard as he feared. She didn't seem to be afraid of him anymore. As long as she didn't invite any other men in for tea. Sheesh, her apparent innocence was mind-boggling.

"Overrun with roosters." Proving her words true, they heard another cock-a-doodle-doo. They both burst out laughing. When they sobered, Ally backed up another step. "Cheerio."

"Night." He stood there as she walked around the corner and disappeared from sight. He wished he had met her in different circumstances. He could really see himself liking this girl.

CHAPTER SIX

ALLY DIDN'T SLEEP WELL that night, and the roosters weren't completely to blame. She couldn't get River and his laughter out of her mind. Were her instincts wrong about him? She'd been wary of him after he tried to scare her on the hike to the waterfall the first day she met him, but when she'd seen him outside her house, her radar had said once again that he was a good guy. She always trusted her instincts, and they were dead on about how her father and Henry were horrible men who would steal an old lady's walker to make an extra pound, but River was their polar opposite. She could see it in his eyes: he was fierce, loyal, and patient. A true protector. She wanted to get to know him better.

Yet why had he been outside her house? Something was off about that. She wasn't sure she believed that his rental was across the street. The other thing that worried her was how well-built he was. Like a bloomin' tank. Maybe he was the guy she'd seen watching her at Wailua Falls. Like he'd said, Kauai was a small island, but it felt like he was stalking her or something. The fear ratcheted up as she wondered if her father had sent him to watch her. The all-powerful duke couldn't have found her already, could he?

Her alarm went off at six-thirty and she silenced it and tried for over an hour to fall back asleep, but the roosters crowing penetrated the walls. She half-smiled as she thought of River telling her it wouldn't help to silence them and she should buy ear plugs.

She finally crawled out of bed, showered quickly, and dressed in an adorable two-piece floral Nani suit—white with colorful flowers, a high neck, and modest enough to cover all but a smidgeon of her midriff. She threw some shorts and a tank top over it. Throwing a couple of water bottles, a granola bar, and her phone and wallet in her backpack, she grabbed her keys and headed to the garage. She liked this rental house with its large windows and modern lines, overlooking Hanalei Bay. Maybe after she'd tried out every hike, waterfall, and hidden beach or cave on the island, she'd relax and just chill on the balcony and listen to the waves ... and the roosters.

She regretted not getting moving earlier as she fell into line on the two-lane road headed to the south side of the island. It was almost two hours later when she turned off the main road and drove up Waimea Canyon. She stopped a couple of times to check out the scenic outlooks of Waipoo Falls. Supposedly there was a hike where she could get a closer view of the falls, but today she had to try out the creepy-crawler hike that every travel blogger said was amazing, seeing the Nā Pali from the Waimea and Koke'e Canyon side. It was supposed to be terrifying with thousand-foot drops on both sides, but Ally found heights exhilarating and she'd never felt the vertigo or fear that some people talked about.

She parked her Jeep at the parking lot near the top of Koke'e and went to admire the view from the lookout before going left to the end of the fence and then around it. It seemed like every spot she wanted to go had a fence and danger signs, but it was obvious nobody listened to these warnings and they only indicated to her that the trail would be more interesting.

The first part of the trail was muddy and treacherous. Ally

hadn't seen much rain, but her research had revealed it rained at the top of this canyon most afternoons, if not all day. This morning was bright and clear, which made her so happy.

She eased her way down a steep slope, but her right foot went out from under her and suddenly she was sliding in the mud. Twisting to one side, she grabbed on to a root and yanked her body to a stop. Her shoulder screamed in pain. Ignoring it, like she'd ignored the ache in her ankle yesterday, she grabbed another root and found a foothold. Slowly, she eased herself down until she was on level ground. She stood and rolled out her shoulder. It wouldn't be too bad.

Glancing around, she realized how lucky she'd just been. Just a few feet away, a ledge dropped off into nothing but green and beauty. "Whew." She tried unsuccessfully to brush some mud off, readjusted her backpack, and started across the meadow and up the next short incline.

She was almost past the meadow when she glanced back and caught a glimpse of a broad man at the top of the incline she'd just slid down. It looked like River, but it couldn't be. If it really was River, then he was definitely following her.

Nervously, she hurried along the trail. If it was River and he was following her to try and corner her, there was nowhere for her to go. From what she'd read, this trail continued along the ridge until it dead-ended on a point with drops on all sides, except the thin dirt path back to safety. They didn't call it creepy-crawler ridge for nothing.

Ally didn't want to go back and face whoever that man was, so she just kept moving, her mind churning. River had seemed like a good chap, but she'd seen him too many places for it to be coincidental. Yes, Kauai was a small island, but not that small. There were dozens of hiking trails, waterfalls, and beaches, and she couldn't think of a single person she'd seen twice since she'd been here ... besides River.

Swallowing down the fear that her father had found her and

sent this too-tough man after her, she upped her pace and pushed through a spot where thick bramble bushes tugged at her legs before coming to a more open part of the trail. The drop-off on her right-hand side was awe-inspiring. She wasn't great with distances, but it looked to be well over a thousand feet.

Her pace slowed naturally as she carefully stuck to the left-hand side of the trail. Even if heights didn't scare her, she respected nature enough to not mess with a cliff like that.

She could see the end point maybe a quarter of a mile in front of her. Stopping to take a drink, she wondered if the man she saw really was River. Then she wondered if she was being a nutter. Maybe he just wanted to get to know her. Not that that justified following her, but it was a much better option than her father sending him.

Turning around, she peered at the spot where the bramble bushes had ripped up her legs moments earlier. If he'd followed her, he was hidden in there. What if it wasn't River but some other man? Sweat rolled down her chest and back.

"River!" she yelled at the top of her lungs. Might as well face the threat head-on, and it was probably smarter to face it here than when the trail had thousand-foot drops on both sides. "Come out and face me like a man," she hollered at him.

He appeared from behind the bushes, and her stomach lurched. She'd been right that he was following her, and he was beautiful ... and very intimidating. He walked slowly toward her, a huge smirk on his handsome face. "Face you like a man?"

She planted her shaking hands on her hips. "Why are you stalking me?"

He spread his hands wide. "I'm not. You have to know that you're a very beautiful woman. I'd just like to get to know you better."

She tilted her head and studied him. His eyes gave nothing away; he'd obviously been trained to not project feelings. A chill raced down her spine. That meant he was either military or private security. She'd been around dozens of men like this paid by her father to keep their family safe. She knew now they probably did a lot more than that, nefarious things she didn't want to think about. She'd thought River was a good person. Her intuition sensor was like a compass near a magnet when he was around.

"You're lying," she spat. "If you wanted to get to know me better, you wouldn't have tried to scare me the first time we went hiking and you would've just asked me out last night." She paused and waited, but his face was like stone. "Did my father send you?" Her voice only quivered slightly.

River kept staring at her.

"Your name isn't even River, is it?"

"Nickname," he admitted.

"Are you military?"

He stared at her for a second, then finally nodded, taking a step toward her. "Ally, look ..."

Ally backed up a step. "You're working for my father." Her throat got tight. Her mum couldn't have ratted her out, could she? Her mum lived to protect her, she knew that, but her father could've done something more horrid than usual. Her mum had sworn to Ally that he'd never hurt her physically, but Ally knew he wasn't above that and her mum wasn't above lying to protect her.

"Your family sent me because they're worried about you," River finally said. "I'm just supposed to keep you safe." He gave her a grin that in any other circumstances would be attractive.

Ally hardly heard anything he said but that her "family" had sent him. She had to get away, and fast. She spun and ran along the trail. Carefully placing each step, she went the only direction she could— away from her alleged protector. No, no, no! How could her father have found her so easily? She would never be free of him. Never. And then the more horrifying thought occurred to her: was her mum okay?

"Ally, stop!" River was calling behind her, but she ignored him and upped her pace.

Her right foot slid and her body tilted toward the deadly edge. She hurried to pull to the left, but that was an impossibly far drop also. Both hands flung out for balance and she cried out as she shuffled and finally leveled out. Ally stopped, hardly able to catch a full breath. Cold sweat ran down her back and her body trembled, pinpricks of fear breaking out on her arms and legs.

Peering over the edge, she felt the bottom drop out of her stomach. She was officially on creepy-crawler ledge and she needed to slow down, but she also needed to get far, far away from her father's hired gun.

River was pounding down the trail behind her. She kept hurrying toward the end of the trail, hating that there was nowhere else to go. The end came up quick and she teetered on a precipice with drops all around her. She sucked in oxygen, terror slicing through her.

A crazy thought echoed in her brain. What if she just stepped off? Heaven was supposed to be a nice place. Her father wouldn't be able to force her to marry Henry and make her life as miserable as her mum's had been. Her mum. Poor, sweet, spineless Mum. Ally was all her mum had.

Crumpling to the ground on the sandy ledge, she broke down in sobs. Why was her father so horrible? Why couldn't she and her mum escape from him? She used to curse her mum for marrying the jerk, for not being strong enough to break free, but as an adult she comprehended how terrifying her father was, how he operated on lies, underlying threats, blackmail, and false charm. He was worse than any politician.

Her mum had confided in Ally once that she'd loved someone else and married the duke to protect her only true love. It had sounded so tragic and beautiful at the time. Now she just thought it was awful. Her mum had suffered endlessly and Ally was destined for the same life.

Strong arms wrapped around her, and she jerked in surprise. Looking up, she saw River had crouched down next to her and enfolded her in his embrace. His arms were so warm and tough it was difficult not to melt against him. Her eyes were bleary from the tears, but she couldn't mistake the compassion on the face that earlier had been stone.

"Ally," he whispered. "Please. I'm not here to hurt you. I'm here to protect you."

"Nobody can protect me," she whispered.

He eased down to sit next to her and pulled her head into his chest. "I can," he insisted. "I promise. I was a Navy SEAL and now I work for the private sector. I was only told to keep you safe and watch out for you on your vacation, but you're obviously terrified of something. Tell me what or who it is and I will protect you and take care of them."

Ally looked up at him. He seemed sincere, but he had no clue what he was talking about. He'd been sent by her father under the guise of protecting her. She could see it all now. Her father hiring River to watch over his "little pumpkin," keep her safe until she was done with her tantrum. Of course, the duke would explain to Henry they'd let Ally have her little vacation, then they'd bring her back home and she'd be ready to assume her responsibilities. He'd probably alert the media too, paint her as the wild child as usual, and show how patient, loving, and understanding he was. She shuddered. Was it wrong to wish a fatal accident upon her own parent?

"You don't understand," she said quietly.

"Then explain it to me."

She couldn't. She shook her head and tried to pull back. He studied her for a few seconds, and she felt exposed and like she'd taken a lie detector test.

"I can't help you if you don't trust me," River said quietly.

Trust. What a word. She only trusted her own intuition, and that had failed her where River was concerned. "You've been hired to protect me." She jutted out her chin. "That doesn't mean I have to trust you."

River's eyes went from a deep mahogany brown to almost the

black of night. He released her from his embrace and she felt chilled, despite the eighty degrees and humidity. Being in his arms for that brief time, she'd sensed how competently he could protect someone and she wished it could be her, but she knew the web of lies her father spun. River assumed he was watching out for the duke's wild daughter and protecting her from herself.

She pushed to her feet and offered him a fake smile. She'd make him earn his pay today, keeping her safe on her adventures, and then tonight she'd figure out a way to escape from him. A sad resignation settled on her shoulders. There wasn't really anyplace she could escape to. Her father had proven time and again that he'd track her down and drag her home by her ponytail, but she wasn't ready to give up, not even close.

"Blimey." She put a gushing note of happiness in her voice. "I guess this means the tough chum is following me."

He stood, and the sheer size of him was thrilling and disconcerting at the same time. She'd always liked strong men, probably because her father and Henry were rail-thin, but this beauty of a man had the power to end all her fantasies of escape. She knew now they were just fantasies, but she'd keep scheming and maybe someday her father wouldn't find her. Maybe if she joined a nunnery in Burma. She'd seen pictures of fantastic monasteries atop desolate cliffs. She could get her mum there too and they'd be hidden.

No. Her father would simply fly a helicopter in and violate their peaceful existence, mowing down the other nuns in the process.

"It would make my job easier if you let me stay close to you." He smiled, but the way he said *my job* chilled her again. She was just a job to him. Of course she was. He didn't even know her, and the second her father snapped his fingers, River would deliver her over without blinking.

She adjusted her backpack and started back up the trail, much more carefully than the way she'd raced down it. Glancing over the edge into the greenery far below, she said a quick prayer of gratitude that she hadn't stepped wrong. She didn't even know how they'd retrieve a body that went off that ledge. Now there was a morbid thought. At least she'd stopped the thoughts of hurling herself from the cliff. Someday, somehow, she'd escape for good.

———

River followed Ally along the trail back to their vehicles and then drove down the canyon after her. He was relieved that she knew who he was and that he wouldn't have to creep behind her any longer, but something was way off about this situation. Knowing her family had sent him had terrified her. He knew nothing about her mom and father, except they were titled Englishmen who were paying a lot of money to keep their daughter safe. Before he met Ally, he'd be inclined to believe she was a selfish and immature girl, but from what he'd seen so far she was friendly, happy, and too trusting. And then she'd done a one-eighty when he told her that her family had sent him to protect her. She trusted strange men but not her own parents? River didn't have the greatest relationship with his father, but he at least respected him and didn't fear him.

Ally's Jeep pulled up to the sidewalk in the small town of Waimea at the base of the canyon in front of a food truck called Porky's. There were food trucks all over the small island and River wouldn't mind trying out a few. Ally bounced out and tossed a grin his way. She was covered in mud, but still breathtaking with her wide smile and bright blue eyes. Her mom was often touted as one of the most beautiful women in the world. Ally was prettier.

River parked a few cars behind her and hurried to catch her as she waited in line.

"Hungry?" she asked.

"Always." Yesterday he'd watched her get fish tacos but hadn't dared stop and get himself any lunch. Luckily he'd had some protein bars in his bag, but that was no substitute for real food.

She glanced up and down his frame. "I bet it takes a bit of food to maintain that. What are you, sixteen stone, seventeen?"

"I have no clue what that translation is." He liked her checking him out.

She shrugged. "About two-twenty or two hundred and forty pounds, I believe would be close."

He laughed. "Closer to two-forty. My mom used to say I ate her out of house and home."

"Were you always this big?"

"Naw. I was really scrawny in high school. Played center for my football team at six-three and one-seventy."

"How did they not break you?"

He grinned. She was really cute. This job was going to be a lot more fun than he'd thought. "Hey, I was still tough."

She licked her lips. "I bet you were."

The couple in front of them stepped out of the way and they moved forward to order. River liked the fun Ally, but wished she'd let him in on what was scaring her so much. He'd have to be patient. He could do patience.

The guy taking their orders had a big smile and a full, dark beard. There were only three things on the menu, so it made ordering easy. River gestured to Ally.

"I'll have the grilled cheese and a water," Ally said.

River looked over the board. "I'll have the grilled cheese, the Polish sausage, the sweet onion chips, and two POGs."

"Hungry guy." The man's smile grew.

"I'm trying to keep up with her." River gestured toward Ally.

Her smile faltered, but she yanked two twenties out and shoved them at the guy. "He never keeps up."

The guy laughed and took her money as River was scrambling to pull his wallet out. "Hey, wait, you're not paying for mine."

She arched an eyebrow at him. "Too late, tough guy. I already got it."

The man in the truck handed her five dollars back, which she dropped in the tip jar. His smile broadened. "She won this round."

River had no choice but to put his wallet back. "I guess she did. I'll be quicker next time."

"Good luck," the guy said, handing them their drinks and the bag of chips. "I'll have the food out to you soon."

"Thanks," River said. He took his cans of POG and the chips and walked Ally to a picnic table, where they settled down.

"I don't want you paying for my dinner," River said again. It grated on him, and his mom would've kicked his butt. She'd raised six boys to be self-sufficient gentlemen with very little help from his father, who made the term workaholic not sound extreme enough.

Ally took a drink from her water bottle and tilted her head to study him, brushing some mud off her arm. He'd almost revealed himself and rushed to her side when she slipped down that cliff earlier, but luckily she'd caught herself on a root. Man, this girl was crazy or brave—he wasn't sure which yet.

"You're a traditional kind of guy, then?" she asked.

"Yeah. Grew up with a big family of boys, and my mom drilled it into our heads that we would take care of and protect others."

"So is that why you went into the military?"

"Part of it." He cracked his POG and took a drink, loving the sweet mixture of papaya, orange, and guava. "Back then I was pretty idealistic." He could just picture himself straight out of high school, thinking he was going to change the world.

"You aren't now?"

He let out a short laugh. "No."

She didn't say anything, and he wasn't sure why he felt like he needed to explain, but there was something innocent and open about this girl, despite the fact she was hiding things from him. He heard himself saying, "In my opinion, there are basically two type of men who go into the military—the guy who wants to rescue the little old lady and the children, and the guy who just wants to kill something legally."

She was studying him intently. "And you were the first, I hope?"

"I used to be." He looked down. "Honestly, it's easier for the ones who just want to kill somebody to deal with the military life, especially when you get involved in Special Ops."

The air felt heavy, and it had nothing to do with the humidity.

"You've seen too much," Ally said quietly.

"That's an understatement." He tried to smile at her but was sure it fell flat. Seen too much, done too much, killed too much. Somebody innocent and perfect like Ally was surreal to him, like a beautiful fairy that would never survive in the real world.

The bearded guy brought their food. It looked and smelled fabulous.

"Thanks," they said at the same time. River was relieved at the interruption—Ally didn't have time to ask a follow-up question about what he'd seen. Some women seemed to thrive on delving into stuff like that, thinking they could somehow cure him. He had no desire to talk about the death and despair, especially times when he'd lost someone he cared about. He tried not to think about Doug too often. Losing that kid had ripped all his tattered ideals out and turned River into a machine that just obeyed orders and tried to get through the day.

The guy stayed. "Sure. I hope you enjoy it."

"You own this place?" River asked, taking a bite of the Polish sausage first. It was stacked with pulled pork and sweet onion. It was even better than it smelled and looked.

"Yeah."

"Wow, it's fabulous." Ally took a small bite of her grilled cheese and smiled up at the owner. "Did you know you're number one on Trip Advisor?"

He grinned. "Must be living right."

"For sure, if you cook this good." Ally winked. "So what can we not miss on this island?"

He looked them over. "From the mud, I assume you like to hike."

River chuckled. "She definitely does."

"Hey." Ally wrinkled her nose at him, then grinned. "Okay, yes, I fancy hiking."

"You planning to hike the Nā Pali coast into Kalalau?"

River didn't recognize the second name, so he let Ally answer. They'd already done the first part of the Nā Pali, hiking to the waterfall the day they met.

Ally glanced at him, then back to the bearded guy. "Maybe."

"It's amazing. I'd definitely recommend hiking the eleven miles into Kalalau Beach and staying a couple of days."

River ate a couple of chips and watched Ally's reaction. The hike sounded exactly like what she'd enjoy, but she was hesitating and acting a little jumpy.

"But be careful." The guy looked over River. "Make sure you take this tough guy with you. There are solid rumors of a fugitive who threw a lady off a cliff last month. The authorities went in to find him but they just ended up busting up the hippies' pizza ovens and driving some of them out."

River's eyebrows lifted, but the news of a fugitive didn't seem to bother Ally. She took another bite of her sandwich and didn't reply to the man's warning.

"Thanks," River said. "I'll watch out for her."

Ally jumped at his words, then quickly ate another bite as if nothing had happened.

"Enjoy."

He walked away and they settled in to savor their food, neither saying much. Ally finished her meal before River, and she leaned back and watched him with a half-smile as he slowly chewed the grilled cheese—also stacked with pulled pork.

"Sorry I'm slow," he said. "This is too good to rush through." He'd rushed through so many meals and he wanted to be done with that life. Sometimes he still felt like that idealistic kid, thinking maybe he could find happiness and innocence with someone like Ally.

She smiled. "It's all right. You full?"

"Almost."

"You got room for shaved ice?"

He sat up straighter. "There's always room for shaved ice. It's like ice cream, just oozes right into the spaces."

She laughed. "We'll see if you're such a big talker in a minute."

"Big talker?" He could out-eat most people he knew.

They cleaned up their trash and waved to the owner as they walked past Porky's and down the street. "I've heard Jo-Jo's shaved ice are mammoth," she said.

"Bring it on."

She smiled at him.

They entered the shaved ice shop and were greeted by some local teenagers with big smiles. "Aloha!" they cried.

"Aloha," Ally returned. "I'd like the colada special." She turned to River.

"Tropical breeze, big kahuna, please." He was ready this time and handed a twenty-dollar bill to the kid before he told them a total.

"Oh, I want mine dakine," Ally interjected.

"Wimp," River teased.

"Ah!" Ally's mouth dropped open.

River laughed and took his change, dropping it in the tip jar.

"Mahalo," the kid said.

They watched them make Ally's first, and it was huge. Intimidatingly so. River was pretty full from all the food at the pulled pork place.

"Cheers," Ally said, trying a bite as they handed it over. "Mmm. That's delicious." She extended it to River. "Would you like some?"

He almost refused, as he could see from the size of her "small" shaved ice how big his dessert was going to be, but she was irresistible. He grabbed a spoon and took a bite. It was perfect, light and fluffy, and the tropical flavors blended perfectly.

The teenage girl carefully handed his shaved ice over the counter. River took it, afraid if he tilted it the entire thing would splat onto the floor. "Wow. That's as big as your head," he said to Ally.

She giggled, and he decided he really liked the sound. This job had changed from a pain in his butt to something fun and interesting in a short time. If only he could get to the bottom of Ally's fears and help her see that he would protect her.

CHAPTER SEVEN

ALLY WAS HAVING a great time being around River, which was crazy considering the heaviness that she felt every time she thought about the duke having found her so easily. Was there any place in the world she could go that he wouldn't find her? She hadn't even used her own credit cards. Had he beaten the truth out of her mum? The thought made her stomach churn, but she kept hoping he wouldn't physically injure her mum. He thought himself so "civilized" and she knew he wouldn't want to mar her mum's perfect face or body.

They drove all the way back around the island, then dropped off River's Jeep at his rental house and he climbed in with her. She punched the gas and headed east back up the hill from Hanalei to Princeville.

"What adventure are we off to now?" he asked.

"You're going to love it," she said.

He arched an eyebrow. "You're pretty wild. Keeping you safe isn't the easiest gig, you know?"

"Oh, poor baby. Forced to play in Kauai for his job."

"Okay. You're right. It's pretty fun."

"Pretty fun? Hiking and snorkeling and exploring and eating yummy food?"

"I didn't get to snorkel yesterday or eat fish tacos, just watch you do it."

Her hands stiffened on the steering wheel. "So you've been watching me for how long?"

"The past two days."

"You're pretty good. I only saw you when you introduced yourself and we went up to the Nā Pali waterfall." It had another name, but she couldn't keep them all straight. "And when I ran into you last night. You weren't just out on a walk."

"I was putting up surveillance cameras."

A shiver ran over her. That was valuable information. She'd have to get away tonight, somehow, someway, before he snuck in any more security measures. Sneaking a glance at River's muscular arms, she doubted she could escape from this bodyguard any easier than she'd escaped from her father.

Ally drove slowly through a residential area and into the parking lot for Queen's Bath. She jumped out of the Jeep and grabbed her backpack and towel.

River followed her through the parking lot and to the trailhead. "How do you know where all these places are?" he asked.

"I studied Trip Advisor and travel blogs for weeks before I came here." She winked at him, but then something froze inside of her. Had her father accessed the IP address? She'd wiped any searches clean and brought her computer with her, but who knew what the duke was capable of?

"Trip Advisor and Google. How would we survive without them?"

"Seriously." She forced a smile at River.

They started down the muddy descent. A few ropes were in place to help them, but they were grabbing on to roots and slipping more often than they were walking easily. Ally didn't care, as she was already muddy from her fall this morning.

"Do you ever go anywhere that's easy?" River asked.

Ally had to laugh at that. "Where's the fun in that?" She slid over a large boulder and almost hyperextended her knee getting down and over the next boulder.

"We've got a perfectly beautiful beach right outside your back patio at Hanalei Bay."

"Yeah, with a hundred other people on it." Ally grabbed a root and slid down the trail on her bum a little way. She was covered in mud and dust. She couldn't wait to jump in Queen's Bath.

"So it's people you don't like?"

"I like people; I don't like crowds."

"Hanalei Beach is not that crowded. You've never been to a California beach, have you?"

"No, but we went to Daytona Beach in Florida on holiday once. Great beach, but wow, it was stacked with people." She and her mum had a terrific time, though: jogging miles along the coast, buying saltwater taffy, riding drift bikes, and playing in the gentle waves. Her father had stayed in their rental house and worked, sending his security personnel to watch them. It had been the most freedom Ally had ever known as a child.

"That's what California's like," River explained.

They made it down the slippery part of the trail and a small waterfall cascaded over the black rocks next to the trail. Ally cooed at the sight. "Oh, that's pretty."

River nodded. "You're a big fan of waterfalls."

"Oh, for sure. I want to swim in every waterfall I can."

"Yeah, I saw that yesterday."

She kept forgetting that he'd been watching her. It wasn't creepy, because River was a solid, good guy, but it was disconcerting. If only he hadn't been duped into working for her father. She knew how military men were. They'd follow instructions. She shuddered, wondering what instructions her father had given River.

They walked along the black lava rock. It was wet in spots and her foot slipped. River reached out to steady her, holding on to her arm for a little longer than was necessary. The warmth of his touch shot safety and desire through her. It was an odd combination in her mind. He wasn't the bad-boy persona that she'd assumed earlier, but he definitely was a kick-butt kind of guy, and she needed to be really careful letting herself give in to the attraction that she felt for him. He smiled at her, and she remembered when she'd given him a quick kiss at the waterfall the first day they met. She'd loved that brief touch of his lips. Shaking her head, she promised herself not to do that again. He worked for her father, and though she suspected he was simply misguided, it didn't matter. He was the enemy.

They didn't say much as they reached the pool, which was separated from the ocean by lava rock. A couple of girls were swimming in the beautiful blue pool. A large wave rushed over the edge of the rocks. The girls were lifted up by the wave, and they giggled loudly. Ally couldn't think about her father while such happiness and adventure lay right below her.

She grinned at River and pulled off her muddy tank top and shorts, keeping her Keen sandals on. "You ready?"

His eyes darted to her abdomen and then quickly away. His cheeks reddened.

Ally bit her cheek so she didn't laugh. He was this big, tough military man, but the way he'd just looked at her was like he'd never seen a woman in a swimming suit. She had to admit, she liked it.

"How do we get in?" he asked, staring diligently at the aquamarine pool below them.

There were a couple of spots around the side to climb in or out, but Ally had read up on this place and she could see the water was deep enough. "Like this!" She ran and launched herself over the ledge. It was only a ten-foot drop, but her stomach swooped with excitement before she hit the water and plunged down. Pushing off the bottom, she surfaced quickly and treaded water, wiping her eyes clean and searching for River.

He peered over the edge at her. "You're nuts," he said.

She put back her head and laughed. The water was peaceful, for the moment. She lay back and floated. He'd join her eventually, or not, his loss. A wave crested over the side of the rocks, and the girls squealed. Ally let the wave lift her body, enjoying the feel of the water around her. It wasn't warm like a swimming pool, but it wasn't too cold either, and her body easily adapted.

She glanced up in time to see River launch himself off the ledge. His splash caused almost as big of a wave as the ocean. Sputtering, she treaded water and waited for him to surface. He came up looking like the warrior he was: his handsome face sparkled with water and his broad shoulders rippled with muscle as he treaded water next to her. A shiver traced through her. He was much too attractive. She had to escape from him, tonight.

"This place is pretty cool," he admitted.

"So you're liking your job of watching over the girl who's 'mad as a bag of ferrets'?" She had no clue if he was familiar with British slang.

He grinned and splashed some water at her. Ally laughed and dodged away. He was a great guy. Too bad she couldn't trust him.

CHAPTER EIGHT

AFTER QUEEN'S BATH, River let Ally drag him to their next stop. They had to park in an unofficial parking lot next to a huge home, and then—of course—they scurried down a muddy hillside with ropes, branches, and roots to keep from obtaining some serious scrapes and bruises. River squinted against the outstanding beauty as they stepped onto Secret Beach, a sheltered half-moon shaped beach with light brown soft sand, greenery all around, and the waves rolling in.

Ally told him her research had said they couldn't swim, body-surf, or snorkel at this beach because of strong currents. He'd developed a sense of appreciation for the power of the ocean growing up on a surfboard and then with the years as a SEAL. At least Ally was smart enough to not mess with riptides. She actually let him relax on the sand and they'd both fallen asleep; afterwards, they hiked to an outlook where they watched whales for almost an hour.

As the sun set they went back to shower and get ready, then grabbed a Luau Pizza from Hanalei Pizzeria. Besides the scare this morning when he was certain Ally was going to plunge off the cliff of Waimea Canyon, and his uneasiness about whatever terrifying thing she was hiding from him, it had been a good day. He liked Ally and didn't think this job would be too tough watching out for her, besides her impetuous spirit and desire to be a little more adventurous than he'd like one of his charges to be.

When they got back to Ally's house, River wanted to stay with her longer, but he didn't want to make her uncomfortable or forget that he was on an assignment. Easy thing to do with a woman this fun and beautiful. He climbed out of the Jeep and smiled at her. "Thanks for letting me tag along with you today."

She smirked at him. "As if I had a choice?"

He shrugged. "You could've just kept trying to ditch me and make me follow you. You were great to hang out with me."

Her smirk turned to a genuine smile. "It was a good day."

"What's the plan tomorrow?"

She winked at him. "We'll see how well your security cameras work and if you can find me in the morning."

River returned her smile, but apprehension churned in his gut. She was going to try to ditch him. The question was how hard of a ditch she was planning. He was beginning to think the issues with her family were much worse than the frustrations and feeling of neglect he had from his father. At least his father was a good person, even if work had always taken precedence over his boys. "You're not going to make this easy on me, are you?"

"Probably not." She walked past him toward her garage door entry. The smell of coconut wafted over him and he couldn't help but appreciate the way her tall, graceful body filled out her simple blue-and-white-striped sundress. She was an exquisite beauty, and he had to remind himself that he was on assignment. Maybe after the assignment was completed he would have a chance to get to know her better. Yeah, right. She was a titled Englishwoman and he'd turned his back on his wealth and a chance to be with someone like Ally. A woman like her couldn't go traipsing around the world rescuing children from human trafficking.

"See you tomorrow," he called.

"If you're lucky," she said over her shoulder. Then she was gone and the garage door slid closed.

River hurried across the road and let himself into his rental house. It was a good deal smaller than Ally's and didn't have the beach in its backyard, but he liked the island feel and the openness of the place. He dialed Sutton's number.

"Smith." It was Sutton's standard greeting.

It made River smile and feel at home. Though Sutton wasn't a warm, fuzzy kind of guy, he was like a father figure to all of them in some ways and he understood the military life and sacrifice better than anybody. Cannon called Sutton "Batman," and it kind of fit—the elusive billionaire who could kick anybody's butt if he needed to—but Sutton reminded River of a mix of James Bond and John Hannibal Smith from *The A-Team*: the craggy face, blue eyes, leadership abilities, and a world of hurt behind his smile.

"I need to know who hired me," River rushed out. "You said Ally's family, but was it her father or her mom?"

"Alexandria wants you calling her by her nickname?" There was amusement in Sutton's voice. His accent made every phone call feel like a top-secret, James Bond mission.

"That's how she introduced herself."

"Getting chummy, are we?"

"I haven't crossed any lines, sir, if that's what you're implying, but she is a wild one. She saw me following her on a dangerous hike and about plunged herself off a thousand-foot cliff when I said her family had sent me."

Sutton pulled in a quick breath but didn't comment.

"She's afraid for some reason." River dug deeper.

There was silence on the line for a few seconds. "It was her mum who hired you." Sutton's voice was warmer than River had ever heard it. "I would never lower myself to work with her father." And now that voice was chillier than ice.

"Okay. Can I tell her it was her mom? She's hiding something from me and she's terrified of someone. Is there a stalker involved we don't know about?"

"No stalker that I know of, but I was hired through a family friend, Lord Kingsley, so I don't have near as much information as I need." He paused, then spoke slowly, as if he knew River needed the information but he didn't like sharing it. "Her father is one of the most vile men I've met, but very few people know that truth. He's the ultimate politician. If Alexandria knows his true character, she'll be terrified of him."

"Thank you for the information, sir."

"Keep her safe, River."

"I will, sir."

"Heart of a warrior," Sutton said.

"Heart of a warrior," River repeated.

The call disconnected and River stewed, wondering about his employer's connection to Ally's family, and not just because they were both from England. He sounded like he cared for Ally's mom but thought her father was a snake. Interesting. He wanted to tell Ally that it was her mom, not her father, who had hired him. Would it make any difference? Would she relax around him and let go of the façade of happiness that she'd shown today? Maybe it wasn't a complete façade. She'd seemed to have a lot of fun today. Maybe she was a master at hiding her feelings like him.

He debated if he should go over and knock on her door, tell her what Sutton had said. How to bring it up, though? *"You were terrified when you heard your family sent me after you. Does it help at all that it's your mom who hired me?"* He didn't think she'd appreciate him bringing up her reaction on the ledge this morning. And what if her mom was as horrible as her father? Poor girl.

His doorbell rang. River stood quickly and hurried through the living area to the front entry. Looking through the peephole, he smiled to see Ally standing there with two large cups in hand. He swung the door open.

"Hey, you," she said. She held the drinks aloft. "I had all the stuff in my kitchen to make piña coladas and wondered if you'd want one."

He stiffened. "That's really nice of you, but I don't drink."

"Lucky for you these have no poison in them." She smiled mischievously.

"What was that?" he asked, gesturing her inside.

She gracefully stepped past him, handing him one of the tumblers. It smelled really good, reminding him of her light coconut scent. "What was what?"

"Your smile. You're hiding something from me." She was hiding a lot and he would get to the bottom of it soon.

She walked to the couch and sat down. "I promise you there's no alcohol in the drinks. I'm not plonkers enough to drink either."

River assumed plonkers meant stupid, but he had no clue. He sat next to her and took a sip of his drink. It was fabulous—coconut, pineapple, creamy and cold. "Thank you. It's delicious."

She took a long swallow of her own drink. "Of course it is. I made it."

"Are you a good cook?" He took a bigger drink this time.

"Yes, sir. My father employed the best chef in the world, and Perry taught me everything about cooking and mixing drinks. Sadly, he didn't know how to bake, so I'm still trying to learn that on my own." Her blue eyes sparkled at him.

River loved good food, and knowing that she could cook made this beautiful woman even more appealing to him. "Wow, that's great. I didn't have the best chef in the world, but my mom was a great cook and she taught me enough to survive." He drank some more of the tropical smoothie. "She had to be a good cook with six hungry boys."

"Six? Wow. I would've loved one sibling, but five might've been overwhelming."

"Naw, it was great. Always somebody to wrestle or throw a football with."

"Boys." She shook her head and sipped at her drink. "Where did you grow up?"

"Long Island." He didn't expound on the fact his family home was a mansion in the Hamptons and his mom was the exception in their exclusive circle of wealthy friends, being very hands-on with her boys and her kitchen. They'd had a maid service that came in once a week to deep clean, but the rest of the upkeep was on her and her sons, and she did a great job teaching them all to work.

"I've only been to Manhattan, not Long Island."

He took another long drink and realized his cup was almost empty and he was starting to feel drowsy. It had been a long day and he hadn't slept well last night, but he had taken a short nap on the beach. "Long Island's much prettier than Manhattan and we have a great surf community. It's not quite as pretty as Kauai, though." He'd fallen in love with water and the ocean as a child on Long Island. The Navy had been the perfect career for him.

"I sure do love it here." She set her cup on the coffee table. River took one last drink and set his cup next to hers. Ally wrapped her arms around her legs and leaned into the cushion, looking relaxed and much too tempting. What would she do if he trailed his fingers through her long blonde curls? She was still wearing the striped tank-top-style dress from dinner. It molded perfectly to her curves. He'd seen a lot of those curves the past couple of days, and it made him feel like a teenage boy with his first crush. "Wish I could just stay here forever," she said.

River followed her example and leaned back against the cushion, kicking his legs up on the coffee table. He couldn't remember the last time he'd felt this relaxed. "Wouldn't you get tired of vacation after a while?"

She elevated one shoulder. "I could buy a beach house and open a food van."

"You mean food truck?"

"Tomato, tomahto. I am British, remember?"

He shrugged lazily as if he barely noticed, but there was no way he could forget with the luscious accent of hers.

"Did you notice Porky's was only open eleven to three? I've seen some places that list their hours eleven-ish to whenever they want to close, and plan on them being closed if the surf's good. That's the life, right? So much better than corporate rubbish."

River could listen to her talk for hours, and he had to admit that life did sound pretty nice. Working in your own food truck the hours you designated, bantering with the vacationers, and surfing, hiking, or exploring whenever you wanted to. Plus you couldn't beat the weather or beauty of Kauai. He wondered if he'd miss security details, though. He shook his head. What was he thinking? His mission in life was to protect victims of human trafficking. Ally had him daydreaming about crazy stuff. His head felt like it was full of clouds.

"Did you work in the corporate world?" he asked, his words slurring. What was going on with his head not connecting to his mouth?

"After I received my master's from Princeton, there were head-hunters offering me positions in some Fortune 500 companies, but then my granddad died and I went home to try to help my mum. I've seen enough of the corporate world my father lives in." She visibly shuddered.

River nodded, sinking deeper into the cushions. He'd hardly sat on this couch before tonight. It was really comfortable. "I'm sorry," he offered lamely, understanding exactly what she was saying. He had no desire to live in his father's world either.

"It is what it is." She brushed him off.

Her father. There was something he needed to tell her about her father. His brain was getting so foggy he could hardly remember. He tried with, "Your father. You said ... how he hired me." He shook his head, but it didn't clear.

Ally leaned toward him, but his eyes were closing. Why was he so tired? She stood and adjusted the pillow, speaking in a soothing voice. "You look knackered. Lay down and I'll let myself out."

She was right. He was tired—that had to be what knackered meant. He should walk her out and make sure she got back to her house safe, but Kauai seemed really safe. He slid down onto the cushion, where she'd set up a pillow for him. Ally pushed his legs around so he was stretched out on the couch. He liked her soft fingers on his legs and it felt perfect to stretch out, to simply lie here.

She stepped back close to his head. He struggled to open his eyes; she was swimming in and out of his vision. So beautiful. So far away. His eyelids drifted shut again, even though he wanted to keep staring at her. He'd only close them for a few seconds.

He could feel Ally lean down close, smell her coconut scent. Had he told her how good she smelled? Would that be crossing any lines? Her lips brushed his cheek, and warmth pooled in his abdomen. He wanted to kiss those lips again. The first time had been much too quick.

"Sweet dreams," she whispered, her breath brushing against his lips.

River arched up to kiss her, but she had moved out of reach. He tried to sit up, but he heard the front door open and close. He was so tired. He'd just lie here for a while; then he'd check on Ally.

CHAPTER NINE

ALLY WOKE to the alarm she'd set for three-thirty a.m. She'd been tempted to leave last night after she'd drugged River, but she knew she needed some sleep and had no desire to cross the dangerous parts of the Nā Pali trail in the dark. Her sleep had been troubled as she worried if River would somehow wake up and stop her from escaping.

She packed up her Cilo Gear Mountaineering Pack with food and water. It already had a small tent, a sleeping bag, a foam pad, and emergency supplies loaded in. She felt a twinge of guilt as she walked out the garage door, programming it locked with the code, and glanced across the street at River's rental home. It was rotten of her to make him that piña colada filled with a dozen sleeping pills. She'd done some research on the internet to make sure that wasn't a dangerous dose for a guy his size. Good thing she'd found out his weight.

It had been her only hope, and it had worked. Maybe her escape from her father would be temporary, but at least she could keep fighting. She was nowhere close to ready to submit to the monster.

The guilt surged again as she thought of River. She liked being around him, he was a great guy, and she prayed she hadn't given him too much ZzzQuil. It was what she used to help her sleep when she traveled and melatonin wasn't cutting it. She'd heard ZzzQuil was one of the safest over-the-counter sleeping pills. Thank heavens it had worked last night and knocked him out.

Ally glanced around, wondering where his cameras were and how good they were. She'd turned out all the lights to mask her leaving, and now she cast one last guilty glance at River's house before slipping around the back of her house and heading along the grassy part of the beach to the public parking lot a quarter of a mile south of her house.

It would be a long day walking seven miles to Ke'e Beach where the Nā Pali coastline trail started. Then it was another eleven miles along a steep and treacherous route to her final destination—Kalalau Beach. She had a permit to take the trail and camp there. With any luck she'd make friends with the famous naked hippies and they'd let her stay with them and protect her from detection for a while. Sure, it wasn't a permanent solution, but it was the best she could come up with at the moment.

She'd googled flights off the island last night and every seat was already booked. She hadn't dared go sit at the airport on standby. River would wake at some point and he could easily track her to the airport. Plus, she only had her own credit cards, and she knew her father had ways to track them. She'd already thrown away the card she used to get here, which he'd obviously tracked.

No, it wasn't a great plan, but she was running from her father and the nightmare of a life he had planned for her. It sounded like the hippies were used to running also. Maybe one of them could help her come up with a plan.

———

River woke to full sunlight streaming through the large windows of the great room area, and he groaned as a headache threatened to split his head open. It reminded him of his high school days when he'd drunk too much and woke up with a hangover. His mom would've cussed him out if she knew he'd ever touched alcohol. She was an extremely religious person and took the Bible literally. None of his brothers were allowed to drink, though River suspected some of them had dabbled in it as well. He'd learned his lesson, though, and stayed far away from alcohol now. So why did he feel so horrible?

He sat up and his head throbbed more. Ally? Had she snuck alcohol into his piña colada? He didn't think so; he would've been able to taste it and she was too guileless to outright lie to him. Maybe she'd mixed some sort of drug in, a roofie? He didn't think an innocent like Ally would have something like that in her possession, and Ally seemed like a sweet, fun girl. What motive could she have for drugging him?

He pulled his phone out of his pocket and blinked at the time. Ten a.m.? He had definitely been drugged, and he was still on West Coast time to boot. It should've felt like noon, but he wished he could sleep for hours longer.

Standing too quickly, he swayed and wanted to sink back to the cushions. Instead he forced himself to his bathroom and swallowed four ibuprofen dry. As soon as he did, he hoped ibuprofen wouldn't mix wrong with whatever drug was in his system. Sheesh, he was going to have words with Ally when he found her.

He splashed cold water on his face, took a long drink, slipped into some flip-flops, and stormed across the street to her rental house. Banging on the door got him no response. He tried the handle, but it was locked. Walking quickly around the house, he tried every exterior door and nothing opened. He stared through the glass doors and windows lining the back of the house—no movement inside.

Easing around to the garage, he was happy to realize his head was feeling better, even though the bright sunlight made him want to shut his eyes and go lie back down. He peered through the garage window and saw her Jeep. Where was she?

Walking around back again, he searched the beach. It wasn't too crowded yet and he couldn't see her blonde hair or beautiful shape anywhere. Hurrying back to his rental house, he cued up the cameras and started scrolling back. A sick feeling formed in the pit of his stomach. He had to find her, and quick.

———

The sky was still dark when Ally made it to Ke'e Beach and the trailhead that marked the start of the Nā Pali coastline trail. It was actually called the Kalalau Trail, she'd heard, but most tourists seemed to call it Nā Pali—it was easier. She remembered how just a couple of days ago she'd taken River up this trail and along the side route to the waterfall. This was the exact stretch he'd carried her down in the dark after she twisted her ankle. Guilt rushed through her again. He was a fabulous guy, but that didn't mean she didn't need to escape from him and everyone associated with her father.

She pushed hard going up the first mile incline, grateful when the sky started lightening and she could turn off and stow her headlight. Rushing along the downhill section, she was grateful it hadn't rained and she could move quickly, but also that she'd beaten the crowds. She arrived at the rock-strewn beach that was the two-mile point and the stopping point for a lot of tourists. Because of her walk from her rental house, this was mile nine for her today. Over fourteen kilometers more to go, she calculated quickly in her mind. Living in New Jersey, she'd gotten pretty used to thinking in American terms of miles for running distances, but she still used kilometers as well. The last half of this hike was definitely going to be harder than the first. Yet the sun was barely peeking over the mountains and she had plenty of time to cross nine miles. All she cared about was making it there by dark.

She shrugged her backpack off and rested it on the rocks above the beach, pulling out a water bottle and taking a long swallow, then eating a handful of sport jelly beans to keep her energy up.

Something rustled next to the trees. Ally startled. She'd thought she was alone. She turned, expecting to see a cat or maybe a blasted rooster, but it was a man ... and he was absolutely terrifying. He was dressed in faded camo with a massive backpack resting at his knees, and his face was gray. Ally tried to look away, but she couldn't figure out what had made his face gray, and she stared like a curious child. Was his face covered with dirt, or did he have some kind of awful sickness? He cracked a wide smile at her, sending her intuition meter screaming in the wrong direction. She forced a smile back.

He waved. "Headed to Kalalau?"

"Yes. You?" Please let him say he was just coming back. She'd read up on this hike and gotten her permit weeks before she came to the island. She'd heard it was quiet this time of year, but doing the hike and camping at an isolated beach with only this guy around was throwing her anxiety out of whack. Hopefully those hippies would welcome her in. Hopefully they were really there. The owner of Porky's had said the park rangers drove some of them out with pepper spray. Her mind flashed to him telling her and River about a fugitive who had thrown a woman off a cliff along the trail. Could this be the same man? *Stop being a scared little ninny.*

"Wherever the winds blow me." He laughed then, and it was the creepiest sound Ally had ever heard—deep and guttural, like a zombie laughing.

She didn't know how to respond, so she took another drink of her water and put it back in the pack, swung her backpack back on, and clicked the straps.

"You've got an early start," the man commented.

He had no clue how early. Now she really hoped she could make it to Kalalau before dark, especially if there were more people like this on the trail or at the campsite. "Yeah. Cheerio." She took off up the trail.

Stopping quick to use the loo, she pulled her pepper spray out of her backpack and clung to it. The loo turned out to be a huge mistake, as it reeked worse than any outhouse she'd ever been in.

Hurrying out of there, she dug in and pushed herself up the next mile incline, checking over her shoulder much too often. Only when she reached the top did she look back down a thousand feet over green cliffs to the gorgeous beach below.

Gray-Face's image wouldn't leave her mind, but she hadn't heard or seen anything, so she warily slipped her pepper spray into her pocket. Was escaping from her father for a few more days really worth the fear of that guy following her? Her intuition was telling her Gray-Face was as dangerous as any person she'd ever encountered.

She shuddered. Maybe she'd traded one horrible situation for something worse. At least her father and River wouldn't hurt her physically.

———

River found the footage of Ally sneaking out of her house just before four a.m., wearing a massive backpack. He quickly googled overnight hikes nearby, relying heavily on Trip Advisor since he knew she used that, and was pretty certain she'd gone for the Nā Pali trail. She'd acted off when the Porky's guy had suggested the eleven-mile hike. Had she been planning on ditching River even then? Was she planning to camp at Kalalau?

River didn't have any answers, but he couldn't just sit here waiting. He had to find her. He didn't have a sleeping bag or overnight backpack, so he just shoved as much dry food and water bottles as he could find into his backpack with his weapons and first aid kit, jumped in his Jeep, and drove to the trailhead at Ke'e Beach.

The first couple of miles were excruciatingly slow as he dodged around hikers in flip-flops and cute little children with sticks for hiking poles. He earned a couple of curse words and a lot of glares, but from what he remembered from Trip Advisor he had eleven miles of some pretty rough terrain to cross, and if Ally wasn't at the campsite at the end ... He didn't let himself think about that for too long.

Failing this mission would be the lowest moment since Doug's death, and he would be forced to make a dreaded phone call to Sutton. But it was more than that. He had to protect Ally. She'd gotten under his skin already, and even though he was ticked at her right now, he couldn't stand the thought of her being in danger.

The river at the two-mile point was low, so he was able to pick his way across the rocks, take a quick glance at the semi-crowded beach, and head up the next incline. Blessedly, the people all disappeared. He was able to jog up and down the next few miles, and because it hadn't rained in days the trail was pretty good. River started feeling some hope that he'd make it to Kalalau before nightfall, and if all was right in heaven, Ally would be there and be safe. He said a prayer instead of cursing like he wanted to. His head was still slightly foggy and ached from whatever she drugged him with last night. This girl was a serious pain. A fun and adorable pain, but a pain nonetheless.

CHAPTER TEN

ALLY HAD MADE it through river crossings and miles of up-and-down terrain, but then she had to creep along Crawler's Ledge. It wasn't as bad as the creepy-crawler part of the hike up Waimea Canyon where River had confronted her, but it was definitely sketchy with loose dirt and a huge drop-off to the ocean below that she couldn't help but focus on. Heights usually didn't bother her, but this thin ledge made her stomach twist with nerves.

River. She kept trying to forget about him and hope she never saw him again, yet part of her wished he was here with her. She wouldn't be afraid of Gray-Face if River was here. She wouldn't have had to walk an extra seven miles with this huge backpack that was cutting horribly into her shoulders and making her back ache if she and River could've driven to the trailhead together and done the hike. It would've been fun to chat him up and ooh and ahh over the beauty and splendor of the jungle-like vegetation and the amazing views of the Nā Pali coastline and the ocean far below.

Her left foot slipped, and Ally cried out and leaned quickly toward the mountain side of the trail. Finding solid footing, she took a couple of long breaths and promised herself she'd stop daydreaming about River. She was almost to Kalalau and the sun wasn't even close to setting. She doubted many people could accomplish what she had today, and she should be proud.

She hugged the mountain and kept moving until she cleared Crawler's Ledge and made it to Red Hill. Pausing to take a drink, she stopped in awe of the view before her. Kalalau. Paradise. She'd seen so much beauty on this island with the lush vegetation, flowering trees and plants everywhere, not to mention rivers, waterfalls, and beautiful beaches and oceans, but this topped them all—the crashing ocean to the right, mossy green cliffs to the left, and an emerald shelf below with the sandy beach stretching beyond that.

She couldn't help but grin. She'd almost made it, and it was the perfect spot to escape from her father and Henry. No cell service. No military. No bodyguards. With a laugh, she imagined Henry or her father attempting to hike in here after her. Her laughter sobered. Would River follow her? There was no way. He would have no clue where she'd gone.

She slowed her pace and simply enjoyed the splendor of the scenery and the peaceful sounds of the waves crashing far below. She made it to the valley just as the sun dipped behind the mountain—tired and sore, but she'd made it. Forcing herself to keep walking to the beach, she saw the shelter and spots to set up tents in the thickly wooded area to her left. She spotted two different camping spots already set up with tents and hammocks, but nobody around that she could see.

Finding her own spot in the privacy of some trees, she eased her backpack off and sighed with relief. That sucker was heavy. She took a long guzzle from a water bottle and downed a granola bar before pulling her tent off the bottom of her pack and quickly setting it up. She undid the thin mattress from under the backpack as well and put it and the blanket in the tent, resting her backpack at the foot. It wasn't a very big tent, but she'd be comfortable in there, and if it did rain, she could at least sleep out of the elements.

Pulling out her towel and a small toiletry bag, she untied her trainers and peeled off her dirty socks. That had felt almost as wonderful as taking off her backpack. She wiggled her toes and smiled at how grimy her feet were. Grabbing a clean tank top and shorts and slipping into her flip-flops, she went to check out the waterfall everyone claimed they showered in. It would be bliss to get clean and sleep. Simply not carrying that backpack and wearing flip-flops felt like heaven at the moment. She paused to glance around at the picturesque beach with the green mountains above and nobody around but her. She closed her eyes and just listened to the waves for a few seconds.

Footsteps. Her eyes flew open. Two twenty-something men were walking her direction, their dark hair wet and only wearing tight underwear. At least they weren't completely starkers. They were both a bit on the gangly side, but they didn't look intimidating, and she was relieved she wasn't completely alone here. All day long she'd half-expected Gray-Face to pop out somewhere and toss her off the ever-present cliffs.

"Hey," the taller one greeted her. "You just get here?"

"Yeah." Ally pushed out a breath. "Can't wait to shower in the waterfall."

He grinned. "It feels great. I'm Rob, and this is my brother, Trevor. Welcome to Kalalau." He stuck his hand out.

Ally stepped closer and shook his hand and then Trevor's. "Thank you. I'm Ally."

"Let us know if you need anything. Our tent is right over there." Trevor pointed, but she couldn't see it through the trees. "But we usually sleep in the hammocks."

"I'd probably sleep on the ground tonight, I'm so tired."

They both smiled knowingly. Ally looked into their clear eyes. She had a good feeling about these two, and she felt reassured that someone else was around if there was any chance Gray-Face had followed her.

"How long have you been here?" she asked.

"We got in last night, heading out in the morning. You'll have to hike up to the swimming hole tomorrow, and maybe if you're lucky the hippies will share their pizza with you."

"They really make pizza out here?"

"Yeah. They'll send someone hiking out just for supplies. I guess the rangers chased a bunch of them out last month with pepper spray and busted up their pizza ovens, but they resurrected one oven. They're interesting."

"But they talked to you?"

"A couple of them chatted with us when we went to the swimming hole, but they didn't offer to share their pizza," Rob said. "They seem pretty harmless, but be careful. You're all alone?"

She nodded, wondering if she should admit that to him, but her intuition said these two were the harmless ones. Yet River had passed her intuition test and he definitely wasn't harmless.

"And how long you staying?" Trevor asked.

She shrugged. "Until somebody forces me to go home."

They both laughed at that, having no clue how serious she was and how she would have to be forced. It was still surreal sometimes that her father had found her and sent River after her.

She said goodbye and continued on to the waterfall. A young couple was there just finishing up washing in the falls. Newlyweds from Massachusetts, they seemed like nice people who simply wanted to be left alone. They didn't offer their names, but Ally didn't care. She was feeling pretty euphoric right now. She'd made a huge eighteen-mile jaunt today, and though she definitely had blisters and would be sore, she felt safe here. As soon as she got clean, she was planning to sleep until the roosters woke her up. Another happy thought hit her. She hadn't seen a rooster since the two-mile point of the trail. Maybe she'd actually sleep all night.

She gazed up at the water cascading down to the pool. When her water ran out she could refill it here, filter it, and treat it. Perfect. It was so beautiful and picturesque. She stripped out of her sweaty neoprene shirt and yoga capris and stepped under the gentle fall of water in her sports bra and boy-short-type knickers. Basically a swimsuit, just a little more comfortable for hiking all day. Nobody else was around, and she supposed Rob and Trevor might be perverts and have come back to watch, but they didn't strike her as those kind of guys. It was getting dark anyway.

The water refreshed and chilled her. She loved it. She stood under the stream for a while, then grabbed her little toiletry bag and scrubbed her hair and body quick with shampoo and body wash before rinsing it all off and squeezing the water from her hair. Being clean after that excruciating hike was bliss. A little food and she'd sleep great tonight.

Stepping out of the pond, she picked up her towel and wiped at her face before wrapping it around her body and slipping back into her flip-flops. Maybe she'd forget putting on the tank top and shorts at all. The locals were supposedly all starkers. Her sports bra and knickers were modest by comparison.

She bent over the pool and washed out her dirty socks and clothes until the pool ran clean. She'd have to hang them up to dry as she hadn't brought much else besides the tank top and shorts and one clean pair of socks.

She heard a guttural sort of growl, and a chill raced up her spine. Ally whipped around. There weren't any predators on Kauai besides the two-legged kind.

She had a split second's worth of panic before Gray-Face tackled her back into the pool. Ally screamed out, but got a mouthful of water instead of a yell for help.

Yanking her back out of the water, he shoved a dirty hand over her mouth and manhandled her to a spot on the dry ground, putting the full weight of his body on top of her. Ally couldn't catch a full breath from the pressure of him and the fear clogging her throat. He smelled of sweat, dirt, and feces, and she was almost glad she couldn't catch a full breath.

She tried to scream out, but only a squeak escaped. Squirming, she couldn't get out from under him and rocks and twigs dug into her back. Her heart raced out of control and she couldn't get any oxygen in.

Terrifyingly, he said nothing. Just pinned her there and kept pressing harder and harder with his hand covering both her mouth and nose. She started seeing black spots and struggled to turn her head and break his grip so she could get some air. If she passed out, who knew what he would do to her.

She managed to get one hand free and smacked his side with all the strength she could muster. He didn't react, just stared at her with his expressionless eyes. His face loomed just inches above hers, providing a good look at his gray skin, so sallow and dirty.

Her energy was already depleted from her arduous hike and her hand hitting him wasn't doing anything. Ally said a prayer for help and tried one more time to buck her hips and move his dead weight. If he didn't release her mouth and nose soon, she would either pass out or be smothered to death.

————

River cleared the most dangerous section of the trail that he'd seen yet—huge cliffs on one side, and soft dirt that was deceptively slippery—just before sunset. He noticed the beauty and splendor of the place, but he was too busy putting one front in front of the other as he upped his pace to a quick jog that he could maintain for dozens of miles. The up-and-down of this trail, the muddy spots from springs or that had never dried out from the last rainfall, and the constant worry of stepping wrong on a rock or off a cliff— it all took him back to BUD/S training. He'd seen imprints of a footprint that would fit Ally's weight and foot length, but he wished he was certain she would be at the end of this trail. Had she hiked all the way from Hanalei Bay and then done this arduous hike? That was almost twenty miles. If she'd done it, she was in a lot better shape than he was.

He finally made it to the valley and then the beach. He only saw three tents in the trees, but assumed there were a lot more people camping up the valley and hidden from his view. One tent had lights on in it, one small one looked deserted, and one had two guys sitting out front in their hammocks.

"Hey." One of them greeted him with a friendly smile and wave.

"Hey," River returned. "Did you see a beautiful blonde—tall, blue eyes, perfect body, great smile?" He couldn't think how else to describe her.

The guy's smile grew. "She said she was alone, but maybe not, huh?"

"She's here?" River almost sank to his knees in relief. He pulled his backpack off and dropped it to the ground.

"Yeah, she headed up to the waterfall." The guy pointed, then looked at him with concern. "You okay, man?"

River pushed out a breath. "Long day."

"Is she your girlfriend?"

River shook his head quickly. "Excuse me." He noticed them exchange a glance as he hurried past them, leaving his backpack on the ground. All that mattered was finding Ally ... and then kicking her pretty rear end.

River jogged toward the waterfall, being careful where he stepped; it was getting really dark with the sun gone. He could hear the waterfall, which didn't sound very big.

As he approached, somebody leapt to their feet and slammed into him. The guy was almost as tall and thick as River. He stumbled back, but regained his footing and pushed the guy away from him. "What the—"

"She's mine," the man growled. "You can't have her."

"Ally!" River drove his weight into the man and slammed him to the ground. Where was Ally and what had this guy done to her?

CHAPTER ELEVEN

ALLY STRUGGLED to open her eyes. Had she blacked out? The pressure of the man was gone and she could hear grunts and the ground-shaking impact of bodies close by. Had Rob and Trevor come to her rescue? She had to help them. Neither of them had any substance to them and Gray-Face was almost as huge as River. If only River were here.

She pushed to a seated position, the world swimming and pain ratcheting through her head. It was so dark, but her eyes finally adjusted and she could see two men wrestling nearby. They were both large men and she knew one of them had to be her attacker. Who was the other guy?

She tentatively stood and stepped closer. The dark-haired guy, who she assumed was her rescuer, had the other guy pinned to the ground. Her attacker was struggling, writhing, and cursing, but not making any progress. Ally felt vindicated that he knew how it felt to be helpless and scared. Yet he was probably too brain-dead to be scared.

She couldn't see her rescuer's face. His back was to her and it was pretty dark, but the muscles in his back, shoulders, and arms rippling under his fitted T-shirt reminded her of River. He pinned the disgusting man to the ground and had the guy's arms twisted up so he couldn't move an inch. Oh, if only it really was River.

Footsteps approached and Rob and Trevor came through the thick brush. Rob stared at the men before glancing at Ally. "We wanted to make sure you were okay with him coming for you." He pointed at the man who'd just saved her virtue and probably her life.

But ... he'd been coming for her? Could it be? "River?" she squeaked out.

He glanced back and his eyes swept carefully over her. "Are you hurt?"

"No," she managed to get out. River was here! He looked unbelievably good to her, but also crazy tough and scary. What was he going to do to her for drugging him?

"Dude," Trevor said to his brother. "I told you we didn't want to mess with him. You military?"

"Used to be," River muttered. "You two have any rope?"

"There are some clothing lines we could cut and bring."

"Thanks. We'll tie him up and hope a ranger comes soon to haul him off."

River was here. Ally could hardly process it. She stood still, simply watching as Rob and Trevor ran off. Her head was clearing and the relief of River pinning Gray-Face down made her so weak she wanted to crumple to the ground and sleep for a week.

"What branch of the military were you in?" Gray-Face asked.

"Navy," River muttered.

"I was Air Force. Respect a brother and don't tie me up. I'll disappear when you let me go."

"I have no respect for any man who would hurt a woman."

"I was just trying to get some play."

"You shut your mouth or I'll beat you unconscious before I tie you up," River told him in a low, menacing growl.

Ally stepped back, semi-terrified of River, but at the same time so impressed with the ease he handled this guy who she hadn't been able to budge. Never in her life had a man protected her like this.

Rob and Trevor raced back a minute later with different lengths of rope and twine. River shifted his weight off of Gray-Face and flipped him over onto his stomach like he was a rag doll. When the guy struggled, River slammed his elbow into his back and the guy flattened to the ground.

"You two hold him while I tie him up," River instructed.

Rob and Trevor came willingly. Rob lay across Gray-Face's upper body and Trevor splayed his body across the guy's rear and legs. River had to work around them and move them at times to get Gray-Face's arms and legs tied together. He cinched him so tight Ally doubted the guy could roll off of his stomach, let alone sit up. She might've felt bad for him if he hadn't just tried to suffocate her.

River wasn't finished, though. He dragged the guy closer to a sturdy tree and used more rope to tie the guy's joined hands and feet to the tree; then he looped the extra twine around his waist and tied that to another tree. Blimey. That guy was going nowhere. Ally wasn't the violent type, but she was ecstatic to see him restrained so tightly. River might be working for her father, but he was a hero and she wanted to kiss him all over his handsome face.

"I think we're good now," River said to Rob and Trevor.

They both slowly stood, looking pretty proud of themselves.

"Thanks for your help, guys." River stood also.

"Sure," Rob responded for both of them.

"You can't just leave me like this." Gray-Face lifted his head off the dirt.

River glanced down at him, no compassion on his face. "You were in the military. You've been through a lot more discomfort than this." He walked away, not waiting for a response. His eyes were zeroed in on Ally.

He looked so good to her, all big and tough and protective, but there was a scary aura about him too. This guy could and would kick anybody's keister. What was he going to do to Ally for drugging him? There was a dangerous glint in his eyes as he strode toward her. It made him even more handsome, but Ally had seen what he'd just done to Gray-Face. Would he hog-tie her as well, then drag her back home?

She backed away a couple of steps, self-conscious in her minimal clothing and worried how River was going to treat her after her stunt last night. Then she cursed herself for doing it. River was here to help her and he had just saved her life. Running toward him, she threw her arms around his neck and squeezed tight.

River's body stiffened, but then he wrapped his arms around her back and held on. "You're okay?" he whispered against her cheek. That touch of his warm breath left her weak.

"Yes. Oh, thank you, River." She gave him another tight squeeze, filled with warmth and comfort from this strong man. His sculpted chest felt like heaven against her and she loved his broad arms encircling her. Pulling back just as quickly, she smiled tentatively up at him. "I'm sorry."

He released her from the hug, but took her elbow and directed her away from the waterfall clearing. "You and I need to talk."

Ally *really* didn't want to talk. Her stomach filled with nerves. How could she explain to him why she'd acted so rash, drugging him and taking off? He worked for her father and she really doubted he'd believe all the rubbish her father was capable of. Nobody but her and her mum knew what he was really like. "I need to get my stuff," she muttered.

He nodded and followed her back to the waterfall. She tried to stay as far away from Gray-Face as she could, but she could sense his eyes following them. The wet clothes she'd rinsed out had been dropped in the dirt, but she didn't care. Self-consciously slipping into her tank top, shorts, and flip-flops, she grabbed everything else and turned to River.

They walked a wide arc around Gray-Face. River didn't touch her again, but she didn't dare not follow his lead.

They walked together to her tent, where she stretched out her wet clothes on a nearby clothesline someone had left behind and stashed her toiletries back in her backpack while River retrieved his backpack and set it next to her tent. River gestured toward the beach, obviously not wanting Rod, Trevor, or the newlyweds, who had never left their tent, to overhear.

Silently, they made their way over the rocks and to the sand. The waves crashed in their consistent pattern. Ally's heart felt like it was thumping louder than the waves as River stopped and turned toward her. His eyes swept over her and he asked for maybe the third time, "You're sure you're all right?"

"Yes, thank you." She forced a smile. "Have a bit of a headache, but ..." Her words trailed off and her eyes widened. How bad of a headache had River had this morning after she drugged him with her sleeping potion?

River smiled wryly. "Yeah. I can relate to that."

"Oh, River, I'm sorry." The words tumbled out. "You've come and saved me and I feel like a git, but I couldn't have you following me."

River reached out and touched her arm. "What are you so afraid of?"

Ally swallowed hard but didn't say anything. She wouldn't even want to start dumping her family drama on him. If he could look into her mum's eyes for ten seconds and see how beaten down and desperate she was, maybe he could start to understand.

"Ally, I promise I would never hurt you. I'm here to protect you. Please don't ever ditch me again."

How could she promise something like that? Even though River had more than proven that he was capable and willing to protect her, he was working for her enemy and he was a military man. He would obey orders and drag her kicking and screaming to her father the second he was ordered to.

"Please, Ally. At least talk to me."

"You aren't even mad at me for drugging you last night," she said, then wanted to bite her own tongue.

River's cheeks crinkled in half a grin. "Oh, I'm plenty mad at you. I'll get back at you for sure. But it's pretty impressive that you could pull that over on me."

Relief washed over her and Ally couldn't help smiling too. The way he said he'd get back at her wasn't like he was going to beat her up and tie her to a tree like Gray-Face. It was like she was one of his buddies who had pulled a good prank on him and she'd better watch out, because there was mischief brewing.

"No one's ever roofied me before." One lip rose in a playful smirk.

"What? No! I used my sleeping pills."

River chuckled. "You are as innocent as I thought." His face sobered. "But I was more terrified than mad this morning, Ally. You disappeared and I took a big chance coming here. What if you'd gone somewhere else and some loser had attacked you and I wasn't there?" He shuddered.

Ally peered at him. For a brief second it wasn't like he was protecting her because it was his job. It was like he actually cared for her. But that was mad, desperate thinking, and she wasn't a desperate kind of girl. She had plenty of men after her. So why did this military man appeal to her like no one ever had?

"Please tell me what's going on," River said. "Why you ran."

Ally took a deep breath and finally settled on saying, "I can't explain to you how things are with my father."

He studied her. "Sutton didn't speak highly of him."

"Sutton?"

"The guy who coordinates my ... work."

"Yet you're both willing to work for the devil."

River blinked at her; then understanding crossed his face. "I didn't tell you last night. I was going to, but then I fell asleep. I told you on that ledge yesterday morning that I came for you because of your family, but I clarified with Sutton before you came over last night. It wasn't your father who hired me; it was your mom."

Ally's chest rose and fell as hope and relief washed over her. She stood stock-still for a few seconds, unable to really comprehend this nugget of freedom and happiness River had just handed her. Her father didn't know where she was. Freedom was still in her grasp. Her mum loved her so much she'd sent someone amazing like River to protect her.

Apparently reading her surprise as confusion, he said, "You aren't afraid of your mom too, are you?"

"No!" She shook her head, and a happy squeal burst from her lips as she threw herself at River.

He chuckled and wrapped his hands around her hips. "I'm guessing that makes you happy?"

"Oh, River! You ... my mum ... oh, I'm so happy!" She planted a kiss right on his lips.

River's lips were perfect—full enough to be interesting but slender enough to meet hers perfectly. River's hands on her hips pulled her in tight and he gave as much as he took from the kiss.

She kissed him for a few seconds and relished in the sparks flying around them. She pulled back, expecting to see fireworks in the night sky. Only the crashing of the waves and the faint outline of the mountains above and the blanket of stars met her gaze, but looking back at River's handsome face, she could almost believe he'd felt the fireworks also. Was it just because of her relief that her mum had sent him, not her father, or was that kiss as special as she'd imagined?

River looked stunned as he stared at her. "You're ... impulsive," he said.

Impulsive? That was about as unromantic a response to a kiss as she'd ever heard.

Ally looked out at the dark ocean. Exhaustion hit her then, as strong as her relief and happiness had been a few seconds before. "I'm knackered," she admitted to him. "I walked an extra seven miles, starting before four a.m. to try to throw you off my track, and then everything that's happened. Do you mind if we sleep, then talk about this in the morning?"

He studied her eyes for a few seconds. "Sure. If you're *knackered*."

"Tired," she explained. "I have a lot to teach you about the Queen's English."

"Good," he said. "It will help me understand Sutton. The other SEALs are always trying to tease him in British slang but I'm not sure they're using it correctly."

Sutton was British? That intrigued her, but not enough to ask.

They turned as one toward her tent and she suddenly grew nervous. Had he brought anything to sleep with? Her tent was not very big. "Do you have ... sleeping gear?" she asked.

He shook his head. "I just grabbed my backpack and some water and food."

Surely he didn't expect to crowd into her tent, did he? Shame rushed over her. He'd rescued her and he was only here because she'd drugged him. If she wouldn't have done that, things would be so different—last night he would've told her that her mum sent him and they could've done this hike together and been fully prepared. They'd be having a great time, instead of him unprepared to sleep and Gray-Face tied to a tree and casting a sick pallor over everything.

"Um, why don't you sleep in my tent and I'll see if Rob or Trevor will let me use one of their hammocks?"

He chuckled. "Ally, I'm fine. Won't be my first time sleeping on the ground."

"It'll make me feel horrible. I got you into this."

He shrugged one broad shoulder. "It's my job. Please don't waste time worrying about me. I'll feel better sleeping outside your tent and keeping an eye on ... things."

The reference to Gray-Face made her shudder. Surely there was no way for him to get free, but she still hated the thought of him being anywhere near them.

All was quiet from Rob and Trevor and the newlyweds as they reached Ally's tent. Ally unzipped it and quickly pulled the blanket out, spreading it on the ground. It was warm enough she could sleep on the pad and be fine.

"Ally." River said her name so tenderly it tugged at something deep inside her, and she wanted to kiss him again. He was tougher than any man she'd ever met, but the way he'd kissed her ... he could obviously be sweet as well.

She straightened and faced him. "You're using the blanket."

He grinned. "You're a nurturer, aren't you?"

Her mum was the nurturer. She was simply a scared little girl who wanted freedom. "Good night," she whispered, then ducked into her tent. Her heart pounded as she thought of River sleeping so close by. Zipping the tent closed, she took a few calming breaths and knelt to thank the good Lord for sending River.

CHAPTER TWELVE

RIVER DOWNED a few protein bars and guzzled a water bottle before stretching out on the blanket and listening to the night sounds. He couldn't hear much past the waves crashing on the nearby beach. If he strained, he could tune in to Ally's shallow breaths. She had to be exhausted from all she'd been through today, but it was obvious she wasn't sleeping yet. He thought about her attacker being a hundred yards through the trees. The guy couldn't possibly escape his bounds, but River didn't like falling asleep with an enemy that close.

His eyes grew heavy despite his resistance—being drugged last night, the hike today while worrying about Ally, and then fighting her attacker were all taking their toll on him. He needed rest badly. He'd sleep for a few hours at least. If he didn't catch some sleep, he'd never keep up with this woman. He smiled, thinking about how cute and impulsive she was. The protective and almost possessive feelings he had for her were more than he should have for a simple assignment. Did Sutton have any clue how hard it would be to stay detached from someone as beautiful, impetuous, and intriguing as Ally? Why had he put River on this assignment and not Cannon? Cannon could've said a little prayer and been able to withstand temptation.

Ally's breathing had evened out and River was feeling content-edly drowsy when the first drops of rain splattered on his forehead. River's eyes opened and the first thing he noticed was the lack of stars. Clouds had rolled in quickly. He knew February was the rainy season, but this was the first serious moisture he'd seen on the island in his few days here. The rain's volume increased and within minutes it was a deluge.

River could've run to the small shelter he'd seen by the beach to get out of the downpour, but he was reluctant to be very far from Ally. He lifted the drenched blanket Ally had spread out so sweetly for him over a makeshift clothesline someone had left, and then stripped off his wet shirt and hung it over as well.

Gently unzipping the tent, he crawled inside and zipped it back up. Scrunched against the tent wall, he wondered what he was doing. There wasn't much room in here and Ally needed her rest.

"River?" she whispered, blinking her eyes open.

"Sorry." He pushed a hand through his wet hair. "It's a down-pour outside. Can I bunker down by you?"

She nodded, her eyes wide as she glanced over his chest. River slid down along the mat. He had to curl himself around her as the tent was too small for him to stretch out. Ally's sharp intake of breath told him she wasn't unaffected by him. He should've been strong enough to keep his distance, but his military life and training suddenly seemed a decade ago rather than less than a year.

"I'm not going to bite," Ally whispered.

"Um ... okay?" Yeah, he really wasn't going to be able to fight through temptation if she threw out lines like that.

"You can scoot closer. I know there's not a lot of room in here for you."

River acknowledged this with a noncommittal grunt. He didn't know what to say, but he wasn't going to kick a gift horse in the mouth. He moved closer to her, so that she was facing him while he lay on his back. Although they weren't actually touching, he could smell her coconut scent and the warmth of her body seemed to seep into him. "Thanks," he muttered.

"Thanks for being here." Ally was so close that her warm breath brushed his cheek. River barely held in a groan as he forced himself not to cross the distance and kiss her.

It was quiet except for the rain assaulting the tent. River wondered if they'd end up getting drenched regardless of their shelter, but it appeared to be holding up so far. She most likely had the highest-quality gear.

He waited for Ally's breathing to slow, but it was coming in quick little pants. Rolling onto his side to face her, he was grateful for the pad underneath him. It was definitely more comfortable than the hard ground had been. He stretched an arm above her head, not allowing himself to touch her. His hand brushed a lock of her silky hair and he sucked in a breath and uttered a prayer for strength.

"Sorry to disturb your sleep," he whispered.

"If this rain doesn't stop, we won't have much to do tomorrow but sleep," she mumbled.

River didn't like the thought of that. He wanted to hike out of here with Ally, report her attacker to the authorities, and know she was safe and sound in her rental house.

She rested her hand gently on his chest, and River sucked in a breath with a loud pop of air. His skin tingled from her tentative touch. That was silly. The military had limited his dating life quite a bit, but he wasn't some loser who had never had a woman touch him, had never felt soft, silken hair against his fingertips. Why did Ally's touch feel so different? Sweet and innocent, yet his stomach was swirling with a delicious heat.

"It's okay to touch me, River," she murmured.

River swallowed hard and almost told her it was definitely not okay. He was on an assignment and he couldn't become emotionally invested. Then he remembered how he'd wanted to kill that filthy man for hurting her. He remembered how hard he'd pushed himself hiking today to find her, worried the whole time that his instincts were wrong and she wasn't here. Having her close was such a sweet relief. No matter the lies he wanted to tell her or himself, he was already connected, invested, and attracted to her.

Slowly he leaned closer and lifted her head up with one hand while he slid his other arm underneath her shoulder blades. She let out the cutest little gasp as he reveled in the feel of her smooth skin. He rested his other hand on her hip. She cuddled closer, and a surge of warmth snuffed out the last of River's exhaustion. He could've run a marathon easily. Her hand trailed along his chest and up to his neck. He trembled from her touch. He should've left his shirt on, no matter how wet it'd been.

Ally arched up and pressed a tender kiss to his cheek. Her breath tickled his lips and he was more than ready to capture her lips with his own. Forget protocol.

"Good night," she whispered before relaxing her face into his shoulder, her breathing quickly becoming long and slow.

Good night? Good night? It was most definitely *not* a good night. He wanted nothing more than to kiss her good and long, possibly messing up the entire assignment. Right then, though, he didn't care about the assignment. If Sutton fired him, he'd swallow his pride and go to one of his older brothers or even his father and do whatever security installments or assignments they needed so that he could keep working with the Panettis to fight human trafficking. All that mattered right now was tasting Ally's lips.

He squeezed his eyes shut. It was too hard with her so close and them facing each other. He forced himself not to roll her onto her back and kiss this tempting woman. *"Good night"* echoed in his head. Even the rain running down the exterior of the tent couldn't drum it out. His chest rose and lowered too quickly. If only he could have one more sample of her lips. Then maybe it would be a good night.

He shook his head and said a brief prayer for help. Maybe his mom and Cannon were praying for him and it would give him strength, but all he could feel was her soft yet firm body close. That delicious coconut scent was going to drive him insane.

———

Ally tried to breathe evenly like she was asleep. River was the one who had come into her tent, without a shirt on to boot, but she was the one who had put her hand on his chest and told him to touch her. He was her personal protector, her hero, and if she allowed herself to be sappy about it, she could admit she was falling quickly for him. She'd dated some really great guys in college, but none of them could compare to River's tough military persona who could also be approachable and fun.

She faked being asleep so she wouldn't kiss him again. His body was stiff against hers and though every inch of that muscular body felt amazing, she wanted to help him relax. She made the mistake of running her hand down from his neck to touch the magnificent muscles in his chest again. She'd never felt something like that against her palm, and it thrilled her.

River yanked his hand from her hip and captured her hand in his where it lay on his chest. "Good night?" he questioned roughly.

Ally couldn't help the nervous giggle that escaped. Her fake gig was up and she loved that her "good night" had ticked him off.

"Are you toying with me, Alexandria?" His breath tickled her forehead.

The sexy way he said her full name sent a jolt of electricity through her veins. "I really like having you close, River."

He blew out a long breath, released her hand, and wrapped his hand around her waist. Rolling flat onto his back, he pulled her into his side, both arms encircling her lower back with a strong grip. She kept her palm on his warm chest and rested her head in the crook of his shoulder. His move hadn't brought her into kissing position, instead it kept her from reaching his face as easily. What she wouldn't give to have him kiss her. She'd kissed him twice now and it was his turn to return the favor. Her body heated up just thinking about it.

"What's your real name?" she asked him when she really wanted to ask him to kiss her.

A few seconds of silence passed before he said, "Channing."

"It's a nice name."

He snorted. "Only my parents call me it."

She couldn't resist trailing her fingers down his chest to his abdomen. Oh, my, he had a lot of nicely formed muscles. His quick intake of breath told her she'd probably gone too far, but she was dying to kiss him and he didn't seem to want to go there. Dang his self-control. "Where did River come from?" she asked.

"I've never been the most ... compassionate guy. When I was captain of my high school football team and the other kids would complain that coach was too tough on them or we worked too hard, I'd steal my mom's expression: 'Cry me a river.'" He shrugged, and her head lifted with the motion. "Someone started calling me River as a joke and it stuck."

"I like it. It fits you."

"Thanks." He cleared his throat. "We should ..."

Ally was the one sucking in a breath now. They should what? She was pretty open to kissing.

"Try to sleep now."

Ally nodded against his bare shoulder, though she wanted to protest. She wasn't tired anymore, but it had been a crazy, long day. She just couldn't resist one last question, though. A question she should keep inside, but it easily spilled out: "Without a kiss good night?"

Silence smothered the tent like a thick, heavy blanket.

Ally had always been too impulsive, but she knew what she wanted and going to sleep without at least a brief sample of his lips would be excruciating. But what if he didn't feel the same? Or what if he thought he shouldn't kiss her because he'd been hired to protect her?

"I mean ..." she started talking when she wished she'd just be quiet. "You rescued me today. You've been great to forgive me for drugging you and running away. I think one simple kiss of gratitude shouldn't be too out of line."

A rumble sounded from his chest, something between a chuckle and a sound of complete frustration.

Ally had no time to react as he flipped her over onto her back, his upper body coming down on top of hers. One of his arms cushioned her head while the other hand cupped her cheek. The night was too dark to see him clearly, but she could feel every inch of his glorious chest against hers and his large palm on her face. Then his lips met hers. This wasn't the gentle kiss she'd planned on giving him to thank him for saving her. This was the kiss of a warrior who'd gone through battle for his woman and wanted his reward. He knew exactly what he deserved and wasn't afraid to claim it.

Ally's arms wrapped around his neck and she returned the kiss with everything she'd been storing up inside her. It was a silent communication of her gratitude for him, the desires he stirred in her, but also she revealed her fears and the sense of panic she felt when she knew the kind of life that was laid out for her. She'd never be free to pursue someone like River—dangerous, handsome, tough, but also fun and kind.

The movement of River's mouth intensified, if that was possible, and drowned out every fear. All she could concentrate on was his mouth, his warmth, his strength. She'd never been so invested in and consumed by someone's touch.

She let out a low moan of pleasure and River smiled against her mouth. His kisses grew slower, deeper, as he seemed to savor and almost breathe her in. Ally arched up and returned each kiss with more desire and joy than she'd ever thought she'd feel in this lifetime.

River drew back, his breathing ragged. "Ally," he murmured.

She lay back against his arm as he gently trailed his hand down her neck and to her collarbone. Ally was gulping for oxygen and hot all over from his touch and his kiss. The silence between them now felt beautiful and warm.

River ran his fingers along her collarbone and then cupped her shoulder with his palm. She was on fire and never wanted him to stop touching her.

"We can't do this," he said quietly.

Cold rejection crept into her bones, even though he was still so close. Ally hated his last sentence. She wanted River. Not only his kiss and his touch, but the knowledge that he was strong, smart, and fierce. That he could protect her from anyone and anything, even if it meant protecting her from his own desires.

Reality rushed over her like she'd been thrown out into the rainstorm. No one could protect her from her father. He would order River killed if he had any clue how Ally was feeling about him. Soon enough her father would find her, and all these delicious feelings and this freedom would disappear.

River carefully rolled off of her and onto his back. He pulled his arm from under her head and crossed his arms over his chest. The tent was small and Ally felt suddenly cramped by his presence. She squeezed her eyes shut, praying that she could sleep and wishing that River wanted her like she craved him. If only he could stay by her side, love her and protect her.

She was a silly, idealistic girl. Love and protection were fruitless quests in her reality. Listening to the rain pound on the tent, Ally blinked back tears and prayed she could sleep and escape River's rejection. Somehow it hurt worse than all the belittlement and betrayal her father had subjected her to throughout the years.

CHAPTER THIRTEEN

ALLY HAD no clue when she finally fell asleep, but her body eventually must've given in to the physical and mental exhaustion of the day. When she woke, the rain was softly pattering against the tent and River was snoring softly next to her. It made her smile. Everything about him seemed so perfect to her, and he snored. She loved it and couldn't wait to tease him about it—

The memory of how he'd responded to that unreal kissing session last night slapped her in the face. "*We can't do this.*" Ooh, she hated that he'd ended their night like that.

He didn't appear to have moved last night, lying flat on his back with his arms folded over his broad, and very bare, chest. Ally rolled onto her side and studied him. Even with his mouth slightly open and snoring, he was the most attractive man she'd ever seen —the defined muscles in his biceps, shoulders, chest, and abdomen, the beautifully formed lines of his face. She felt like she knew him so well. When he smiled, a slight depression appeared in his left cheek. It wasn't a dimple, but it gave him character. He cared deeply about her, but he wouldn't allow himself to develop a relationship. He was strong mentally and didn't let many people close to him. He was a good person clear through. It turned out her intuition had been right about him all along, despite her doubts.

As she watched him, he shifted and blinked a couple of times. His head twisted quickly to the side, catching her staring at him. He smiled slightly. "Hey."

"Hey," she whispered, still staring. If it made him uncomfortable, he could get out of her tent.

He rolled onto his side so he was facing her. They were close in the small tent and she was half-tempted to kick him out into the muddy, gray morning. Jerk didn't want to kiss her anyway. She smiled at her immature attitude. She owed him far too much to not treat him nice.

"Did you sleep?" he asked.

"I did. No roosters to wake me up."

He grinned at that. "The rain's not as bad."

"No."

They lay there, staring at each other. She loved the deep brown of his eyes and the long lashes framing them. Why, oh why had he stopped kissing her last night? Why, oh why was she daring to think she could love someone like River? Her miserable future was set and there would be no Rivers to heat her up or make her smile.

She broke the connection, sitting up and grabbing her backpack from its spot at her feet. "Hungry?"

"Always." He sat and stretched his arms above his head. Ally made the mistake of glancing at him and dropped the snack packs of dried fruit she'd fished out of her bag. She averted her gaze from his chest and grabbed the bags, tossing one at him, then handing him a water bottle.

River's fingers brushed hers as she handed over the water bottle, and her stomach smoldered. Sheesh, she was pathetic. It was just a quick touch. She pulled out a large bag of almonds, unzipped it, and offered him some. They crunched their breakfast with only the rain for accompaniment. Ally didn't know what to say to him, besides demand he tell her why he stopped kissing her last night. Why they *"couldn't do this."*

Ally drained her water bottle and crumpled it up, putting it back in her pack along with the wrapper for her dried fruit mix. She pulled out some tissue. "I need to ... find the ladies' room."

River chuckled. "I doubt the accommodations are going to be what you're used to."

Ally glared at him. "I'm not some prissy rich girl."

"You've proven that," River said, lifting his hands in defense. "I just meant the bathrooms I saw looked pretty sketchy."

What were her options? Go out in the bushes and pray somebody like Gray-Face didn't come along? "I'll take my chances," she said.

"I'll come with you." River grabbed another handful of nuts and unzipped the tent flap. He ducked out the opening, sliding into the wet shoes he'd left sitting outside.

Ally cringed at the sound of his squishy, wet shoes as she carried her flip-flops out and slipped into them. River hadn't been prepared to stay here and he obviously wasn't prepared for rain. Now that she knew it was her mum who had sent River, and after being attacked by Gray-Face, she didn't want an extended stay in this exotic remote wilderness either.

Rain softly fell on her hair and face as she stretched her arms above her head. Her legs were definitely stiff from yesterday, but besides some blisters on her heels she felt pretty good. She turned slowly, drinking in the greenery around them, until she saw River watching her. Quickly lowering her arms, she tugged her tank top back over her abdomen.

He glanced away and gestured toward the spot for the loos. "Why don't you use the bathroom while I check on ... your attacker."

She nodded and hurried away from him, glad he wasn't going to stand watch too closely, and *really* glad she didn't have to see Gray-Face yet.

River was right about the loo being "sketchy." Ally held her breath and tried not to think about germs as she finished and hurried out of the composting toilet station. Grateful she'd remembered hand sanitizer, she left the small bottle by the loo for others to use.

She could see River, Rob, and Trevor over by the waterfall. Slowly walking that direction, she tried not to look at Gray-Face, but found her eyes drawn to the ground where he lay, looking miserable. She felt a tiny dart of pity for him, but not enough to insist they change his situation. His face wasn't quite as gray today; the rain had given him a much-needed bath. At least the tree River had tied him to had given him some protection.

Rob and Trevor were talking with River, none of them looking at Gray-Face. Ally walked up to River's side and he glanced at her. "They're saying we can't hike out of here today."

Rob raised one shoulder and hand. "You could try it, but it'd be miserable and you're already getting a late start. We were going to head out today too, but I can't imagine Crawler's Ledge muddy." He shuddered. "Also, the rangers will shut the trail down from the other side with this much rain. Crossing the rivers when they're swollen can be really dangerous."

River nodded and glanced up at the sky, which was more of a mist now. "The rain looks like it's clearing." He focused on Ally. "Will you be okay if we stay one more night? Hopefully it'll dry out tonight and we can get an early start tomorrow and take it slow."

"I was planning on staying for weeks, so yeah, I'll be fine."

River gave her half a smile. "I changed your plans?"

"You're brilliant at doing that," she shot back.

"I'd happily do it every day."

Ally's jaw dropped and she had no comeback.

Rob whistled. "Okay, while you two flirt we're going to go pick some fruit for breakfast."

The newlyweds walked into the clearing before Rob and Trevor could leave, and their eyes widened. Newlywed guy said, "What's going on here?" He was obviously uneasy and stepped in front of his wife, gesturing toward Gray-Face yet keeping his eyes on River. "You can't just tie somebody up like that and leave him in this weather."

River turned to face Newlywed Guy in all his bare-chested glory. It took Ally's breath away. He would look pretty intimidating if you didn't know him. "He tried to kill …" River paused.

Ally wondered if he was trying to figure out what to refer to her as. "My assignment"? "My kissing partner"? "My pain in the tush"?

"Ally." River gestured toward her.

"I wasn't going to kill her," Gray-Face grunted out.

Ally couldn't help but shiver at his guttural voice. She hadn't heard him talk since last night, and she wanted to be far, far away from him. Newlywed Guy looked even more uncomfortable.

"I was trying to make her pass out so I could take advantage of her without her screaming for help," Gray-Face finished his explanation, as if that made everything better.

Ally stepped closer to River. He put his arm around her waist and she leaned into him. All the terror of being attacked rushed over her again.

Newlywed Girl grabbed her husband's arm, looking sick. Newlywed Guy glared at Gray-Face, then turned back to River. "Yeah, you have every right to keep him tied up. Did you notify the authorities?"

"How?" River asked.

"Oh …" Newlywed Guy must've realized how stupid his idea was. "I guess one of us should hike out and let them know."

"We'll go tomorrow morning," River said. "If the rain stops."

"Okay." He and his wife walked a wide arc around all of them and filled up the water containers they'd brought with them.

River glanced down at Gray-Face, then looked to Rob and Trevor. "Do you guys mind giving him a little food and a drink?"

Trevor drew back like he didn't want to get anywhere near the man, but Rob nodded. "No problem."

River kept his arm around Ally and escorted her away from the group. She really appreciated his support right now.

"Should we go find the swimming hole?" she asked as brightly as she could manage.

River glanced swiftly down at her. "You're up for exploring?"

She was up for anything that got her away from thinking about or seeing Gray-Face. Nodding quickly, she said, "From what I read, you just follow the trail up the valley and there's a great swimming hole, maybe half a mile. If we're lucky, we'll find the hippies and they'll share their pizza."

"Pizza?" River smiled, but then his expression fell. "Are there really hippies here?"

"Apparently they live up the valley," she said as they reached the tent. "I'd planned to ask them to shelter me, until you told me it was my mum that sent you, not my father." She looked away from his compassionate gaze and said, "You'll fit right in. I hear they're starkers."

"Crazy?"

"No." She laughed and gestured to his bare chest. "Naked."

River grinned at her.

Her face flushed. "Do you mind if we take your backpack with some water and snacks? Mine's pretty huge to carry on a day trip."

"Sure." He pulled a few things out of his backpack and then slung it onto his bare back.

"Sure you don't want to put your shirt on?" She looked at his chest, then looked away quickly.

"Naw, I'll let it dry. Unless I'm making you uncomfortable?"

She glanced back at him and wanted to kiss the smart-alecky grin right off his face. "Just didn't want the backpack to cause you any chafing."

He lifted his chin at her. "Yeah," he drawled. "That was exactly what you were worried about."

Ally rolled her eyes, ignoring his smirk, and crawled into her tent to grab her dry pair of socks. Sitting on a rock, she put her socks and wet shoes on. The day was still dreary, but at least the rain had stopped.

When she stood, River gestured toward the trail that led up the valley. She took the lead, and they plunged into the thick forest. Ally slowly traversed the muddy trail, glancing at all the greenery and nature's beauty around them. They followed a stream for a while and eventually found a large swimming hole. Bushes and trees surrounded it and a small waterfall trickled in from one side.

Ally clapped her hands. "It's so perfect!"

River chuckled, shaking his head and setting his backpack down.

Ally glared at him. "What?"

"Nothing." He shook his head and met her gaze. "You're just really ... cute." He smiled at her, and the sun seemed to break through the clouds for a minute.

Ally blinked in surprise, but River had already bent down to untie his shoes. Though it was warm outside, the sun was still hidden. She needed to stop being so affected by everything he said, and every look he gave her, and the perfect muscles showcased in his back and arms as he bent over.

She followed his example, slipping off her shoes, then quickly peeled off her tank top and shorts and jumped over the small ledge into the pool. River slid in after her. She treaded water, staring at the beauty around her, most especially one hunk of a man who was treading water so close by. He smiled at her, and she returned it. He thought she was cute? He'd said it like he thought she was fun and interesting, not just physically cute. Did that mean he might like her a little bit? Did that mean she wasn't just an assignment to him?

Breaking from his gaze, she leaned back and floated, staring up at the trees and the cloudy sky. She was getting much too invested in River. Soon they'd get back to real life and all of this would fade into a wonderful dream. Before she knew it, she'd be back under her father's rule and forced into marrying Henry. She shuddered, thinking about Henry. If only dreams could come true and River could be the one her father forced her to marry.

Ally sighed. As long as she was hidden in this paradise, she was going to savor every minute of it, especially every look, touch, and kind word River gave her.

———

River watched Ally float on her back. Did she have any clue how beautiful she was? Her long blonde hair looked darker in the water and floated around her like a halo. Her perfect facial features and perfect body looked relaxed and much too tempting to him.

He forced his gaze away, and saw movement in the trees. Suddenly alert, he fixed his attention in that direction. There it was again. Definitely a person.

He touched Ally's side, prompting her to open her eyes and lift her head. "We've got company," he whispered.

Ally treaded water by his side, and he could feel the tension radiating off of her.

"It's okay," he said soothingly, but he was uneasy.

Maybe it was simply because Ally had been attacked last night, but he felt like he was back in the Philippines with locals or Al-Queda eyeing him suspiciously from behind the lush trees. Once the locals got to know him and his squadron, the Filipino people were very generous and taught him more about being happy than even his own mom had, but this still reminded him of that feeling. He was on someone else's property and they were watching him carefully.

"Let's get out," he murmured to Ally.

She nodded.

He vaulted onto the rocks and offered her his hand without turning his back on whoever was out there. He lifted Ally out and ushered her behind him. They walked slowly to where they'd left his backpack and her clothes. Before Ally could pick up her tank top, a low voice said from the bushes, "Don't get dressed on our account, pretty girl."

River pushed her behind him, holding on to her waist with one hand. Ally trembled under his touch. "It's okay," he reassured her, before his eyes narrowed and he looked at the bushes. "Come on out," he called. "We'd love to meet the hippies of Kalalau." He'd really *love* to meet them head-on. Hippies were peaceful people, "make love not war" and all that crap, right? He actually hated hippies. The type of people that protested the military and had no clue that all of their freedoms to act like idiots were protected by heroes like Doug laying down their lives for them. He wished they all would be sentenced to live in a village in Afghanistan for one year and see what it was like to have no freedom.

Several young men sauntered out of the trees. Every one of them completely nude and pretty scrawny. River could take all of three of them at once and not worry too much about the outcome. The guy in front had blond dreadlocks and a big grin on his face. "Hippies? Is that what they call us now?"

"Yep. What do you call yourselves?"

"Locals."

They sounded Hawaiian but looked like Americans to River.

Dreadlocks tilted his head like he was trying to peek around River. "Why are you hiding the beautiful woman?"

"She's shy." He gestured to them. "You're making her uncomfortable."

They all laughed at that. "Sorry, pretty girl," said the youngest-looking one with short, dark hair. "You strip too and we'll all be more comfortable."

Ally broke from River's hold and came around to his side. "No thanks." She tilted her head and gave them a challenging glare, then walked over, grabbed her tank top and shorts, and tugged them on.

All of them, River included, watched her. He'd told her earlier she was cute, but that had more to do with how fun and unique she was. The truth was that between her lean body and her womanly curves, she was exquisite.

River cleared his throat. "So you live here?" he asked the men, hoping to break their concentration from Ally.

"We've been here a few months," the one with the blond dreadlocks said, looking at Ally like a teenager seeing a supermodel in real life.

Ally walked back to River's side, and he smiled down at her before focusing on the "locals" again. She reached for his hand and gave it a squeeze. His heart felt like it was bursting at her simple move. He wanted to keep her by his side and protect her from idiots like this hitting on her.

"What about you?" the tall one asked.

"Just got here last night."

"Short-timers?"

"Yeah." River kept his focus on their faces. He really didn't need to see another man naked. "Word is you guys make pizza?"

They all grinned and nodded.

"Where do you get the supplies?" His stomach was rumbling just thinking about pizza. Any real food would be fabulous, actually.

"We send someone out for them, or sometimes a boat will bring supplies in."

"You need money to pay for that." River inclined his chin. "I'll give you a hundred bucks for a pizza."

The dreadlocks guy roared at that. "We don't need your money." He focused in on Ally with a puppy-dog-looking grin on his face. "We'll give the pretty girl all the pizza she wants ... as long as she doesn't share it with you."

River wasn't sure how his offer to pay had offended them. "Hey, I didn't mean to upset you."

"Well, you did, military man." The dreadlock guy had lost his smile and was glaring openly at him now.

River released Ally's hand and folded his arms across his chest, knowing it was intimidating but not caring. "How'd you know I was military?"

"You just have that stick-up-your-butt look," the young-looking one said, snickering. "You going to try to arrest us for not having permits? Maybe you brought your pepper spray to try to chase us out?"

"Naw." River arched an eyebrow. "But I'll kick your trash for nothing."

"You wish," the tallest one countered.

"River," Ally whispered. "There are three of them."

"Probably more than three." He pulled Ally into his side and ushered her with him toward his backpack while the men watched them, saying nothing. River grabbed his backpack and pulled out a Bowie knife and his favorite 1911 pistol. He'd had to declare them and check them at the airport, but it was more than worth it to have his weapons with him.

"River." Ally stepped away from him. Her eyes widened and he couldn't tell if it was fear or admiration that filled them.

He gave her a fleeting smile and turned back to the men.

"So you need weapons to fight us?" the dreadlocks guy asked.

"I could take you three with nothing, but you tell all your buddies not to mess with us and *you* stop checking out my girl. Got it?" River's neck was hot and he felt an urge to drop his weapons and kick all of their butts in hand-to-hand combat just to relieve the anger building inside of him. He hated people who thought they were above the rules and could take anything they wanted. None of them had better make one more crack about the "pretty girl."

The dreadlock guy nodded slowly. "Loud and clear, military man." They looked unnaturally solemn as they melted back into the trees.

River released his clenched grip on his weapons and carefully stowed them back in his backpack. He pulled out a couple of granola bars. "Hungry?" he asked brightly.

Ally stared at him, her blue eyes wary. "River ... what just happened?" She sank onto a rock, shaking her head.

River dropped the granola bars and his backpack. He crouched in front of her and took both of her hands in his. "It's okay. They won't dare came after us now."

"That escalated really quick. I don't think they meant us any harm." Her hands trembled.

"You're right. I probably reacted wrong, but I just ... hated the way they were checking you out."

Ally leaned back. "That's why you acted like that? All alpha male, 'I'm the military hero who's going to slit your throat'?"

River chuckled. "Come on, I wasn't that bad."

"You were." She stared at him and shook her head. "You were terrifying. I thought the youngest kid was going to pass out he was so scared."

River stood and tugged her up. "Good. Then they won't mess with us."

She let out a little laugh, and River hoped that meant she wasn't scared of him. "One thing's for sure."

"What's that?"

"You aren't getting any pizza today."

River groaned and his stomach rumbled as if on command. "Ah, don't remind me." He had to force himself to step back and release her hands. She was so cute to him right now. Okay, she was cute to him all the time. How was he going to keep from kissing her again? "As soon as we hike out of this hole, we're going for pizza."

Ally gestured around at the splendor of lush forests, mountains, streams, and waterfalls. "This hole?"

"It's beautiful, but I really like flushing toilets and real food."

Ally gave him a genuine laugh then. "Wussy military man."

He joined her laughter, even though it was at his expense. She could probably guess that he'd been in much more dangerous and uncomfortable situations than this, but between her attacker and these hippie guys giving him bad vibes, he wanted out of here as soon as it was safe to hike. He was going to pray hard tonight for no rain.

"Let's get out of here." He picked up his backpack and swung it back on.

"Are they still watching us?" she whispered.

"No. I can't feel anybody, but like you said, I'm not really doing a good job of winning friends in this valley."

"No, you're not." She started down the path and he followed. Glancing over her shoulder at him, she winked. "But you only need one friend."

"Can that friend be you?" As soon as he'd asked it, he wished he hadn't made himself so transparent with that line and calling her "his girl" to the hippies. He'd been so proud of himself when he'd been strong enough to stop kissing her last night. It had been torture, but he needed to get her out of here safe before he could explore more of a relationship with her.

"Maybe." She grinned, then picked her way down the trail. River followed her closely. If she was his only friend, he'd be happy with that.

CHAPTER FOURTEEN

ALLY'S FEELINGS about River ping-ponged around from being in awe of him, being attracted to him, and really enjoying being with him, but then there was the sting of him ending their kisses last night and the fear of his ability to kick anyone's butt anytime he wanted. Why was he so patient with her? She'd drugged him with sleeping pills and he'd forgiven her easily. Those hippies had looked at her cross-eyed and he'd threatened to dismantle them.

They didn't talk much as they slowly made their way along the muddy trail back down to the valley. River stopped and picked mangoes for them and they devoured those before moving on, neither of them in a hurry to return to the campsite and sit and wait until night fell.

Ally really hoped it wouldn't rain again. She agreed with River that she'd be happy to hike out of here tomorrow and get back to real food, toilets, beds, and a shower. More than that, the hippies had made her uncomfortable with their nakedness and hitting on her, even before River started threatening them, and she wanted to be far away from Gray-Face. She trusted the bonds and was confident he couldn't escape, but just being around him felt like a black cloud.

As they arrived back at the beach, they walked past the waterfall. Ally didn't want to even see Gray-Face, but she could understand why River felt like he needed to check on him.

Ally looked around, blinked, and scanned the area once more. It couldn't be possible. "Wh-where is he?" she asked.

River's face was hard and his eyes flashed angrily. He rushed over to the spot Gray-Face had been and started sifting through the rope and twine lying there. "Cut," he muttered. Then he picked up a couple of pieces of pizza crust. His eyes widened, and he cursed and chucked the crusts at the waterfall.

Ally backed instinctively away. River looked angry enough to disassemble someone. He stood and stormed toward her. "Don't leave my side," he commanded.

"Okay." Fear rushed over her at his words. Gray-Face had escaped and the hippies had obviously helped him. They must've known a shortcut to camp, but why would they untie Gray-Face? The guy had almost taken advantage of Ally, and he definitely had to hate River for tying him up and leaving him exposed to the elements all night.

River took her elbow and they walked quietly through the woods and to the campsites. Rob and Trevor were sitting in their hammocks.

Rob looked up at them first. "Hey. How was the swimming hole?"

"Did you see anybody cut the fugitive's ropes?" River demanded.

"What?"

"The guy who attacked Ally."

They both stood, their eyes wide and obviously a little afraid at the anger radiating from River. "He's ... gone?" Rob asked.

River strode up to them, stopping a foot away. Ally stuck by his side.

"If either of you helped him escape and think you can lie to me about it, I will ..." He glanced swiftly at Ally. "Let's just say it won't be pretty."

Rob swallowed, his Adam's apple bobbing. Trevor took a step back, lifting his hands up. "I promise, man, we would never let that guy go. Promise."

River studied them each carefully for a few seconds. "Where are the newlyweds?"

"They've barely left their tent all day," Rob gushed out. "Not sure why they hiked all the way in here to ... just stay in their tent."

River arched an eyebrow but didn't comment.

Ally touched his arm. "It had to be the hippies—the pizza crust."

His face hardened again. A muscle worked in his jaw as he studied her. "You're right." He blew out a breath and rolled his shoulders back.

"Are the hippies dangerous?" Rob asked. "They were pretty chill with us when we saw a couple of them up the valley."

"I don't think they're dangerous," River admitted. "But they don't like me and they probably released him just to tick me off."

"Did you read up on any of the stories online before you came out here?" Trevor asked.

River shook his head.

"They claim there's a fugitive on the loose who is wanted for murder and also threw some lady off a cliff out here."

River blinked at him, then turned to Ally. "The Porky's guy told us about that."

Rob lifted his shoulders. "You can't believe every story, right?"

"I wonder if Gray-Face is the fugitive." Ally shuddered at the thought.

"Gray-Face?" River turned to her.

"That's what I nicknamed him the first time I saw him."

"You saw him before he attacked you last night?"

"Yeah. At the two-mile beach. You know, hankapappi-ee-a or whatever."

River actually smiled at her, but his seriousness came back quick.

"What should we do?" Rob asked.

River glanced up. The sun was breaking through the clouds, but it had to be early afternoon with as late as they'd slept and their hike to the swimming hole. "We don't dare hike out of here today. Going over a muddy crawler's ledge and getting stuck on the trail in the dark would be stupid. Let's move the tents close together, up against the mountain. We'll take turns watching tonight, then pack up and hike out first thing in the morning."

"Okay," Rob agreed for both of them.

River started issuing instructions and they all listened carefully. Ally felt like she was part of some lost-in-the-woods survival movie, and was only reassured by River's confidence, strength, and the calm way he instructed everyone.

As Rob and Trevor hurried off to talk to the newlyweds and then break down their camp, River turned to her. "I meant what I said earlier ... don't leave my side."

Ally glanced over him. This man would protect her. "I don't plan on it."

He squeezed her arm. "It's going to be fine. Sorry I riled the hippies up."

Ally tried not to think about Gray-Face out there, watching them, possibly riling the hippies up even more. "Sorry you don't get pizza for dinner."

He flashed a smile. "I'll be taking you out for pizza tomorrow night."

Ally really hoped he was right.

———

River was on edge as darkness fell. He touched the knife he had strapped to his cargo shorts. His pistol lay next to him on the ground; it had been cutting into his back when he had it jammed into his belt there.

The afternoon passed fairly quickly as they set up a defensive spot next to the mountainside with the three tents. The newlyweds —Ty and Claire—had warmed up to them and talked with the rest of the group. Nice couple, really. They just wanted to be left alone. River stole a glance at Ally, seated on the ground next to him. The two of them were leaning against her large backpack. He empathized with the newlyweds, thinking of how he'd love to be alone with her.

They finished eating a decent meal that mostly came from Ty and Claire's supplies, wrapped up the garbage, and stored it in their packs. Ty and Claire claimed they didn't want to haul all the food out and had agreed to leave tomorrow as well. The rain must have kept anyone from coming in today; apparently the rangers had shut down the trail. Ty also explained that this was a slow time of year because it was the rainy season and not an official vacation break for a lot of people, but there could be as many as sixty campers with permits so more people could easily be coming tomorrow. River itched to get out of here and report Gray-Face, as Ally called him, to the authorities and explain that the hippies had cut him loose. He imagined there was a good deal of animosity between the rangers and the hippies anyway, and maybe he shouldn't add fuel to the fire, but those guys ticked him off.

He looked around at the group. Rob had been telling Alaska deep-sea fishing stories to Ty, but their conversation had petered off and everyone was pretty quiet. River felt like the entire group was his responsibility, and he knew it was on him that the hippies had gotten mad and come down to their camp and cut Ally's attacker loose. His blood was still boiling at the memory. The way they'd stared at Ally. The way they thought they were above the law. The way they denied him pizza.

The problem was he didn't know if they would try to attack

their little group and he had no clue if there were three of them or three hundred. Would Gray-Face rile them up, or had that loser already taken off? The hippies were probably all doped up and sleeping in their tree forts, and River was being way overcautious and over-worried.

"Should we start a fire?" Claire asked.

"No fires." River shook his head. "We'd be blind and they could see every movement we make."

She shrank back against her husband. River pushed a hand over his face. He'd made this into a war zone and none of these people had signed up for this. He glanced at Ally again. She looked up at him with such trust in her eyes. Ally hadn't signed up to be attacked and River had every right to whip that guy for it. He'd been a little defensive with the hippies, true, but that didn't give them any right to cut a guilty prisoner free.

"Why don't you all get some rest?" River tried to use a gentle voice. "I'm sure there's nothing to worry about, but I'll stay up and watch just in case."

"You're going to stay up all night?" Rob's brow wrinkled.

River tried not to laugh in the kid's face. He better never join the military. "It's not a big deal. I've done it before."

Rob and Trevor exchanged a look. "Well, you don't need to do it alone. We'll each take turns watching with you."

River opened his mouth to protest.

"Good idea," Ally interrupted him. "I'll take first watch with River. Then I'll wake Rob up and you can each take a turn through the night."

They all nodded, said their good nights, and climbed into their tents. Ally sat quietly by his side for so long it was making River uncomfortable, and he usually never minded silence.

He listened intently and could hear the soft breathing of their new friends barely over the crashing of the waves. Glancing down at Ally, he could make out her features with the starlight and a sliver of a moon for help. At least it wasn't raining tonight and they could hike out of here tomorrow.

"You don't have to sit up with me," he said.

She tilted her chin up. "You don't have to be the superhero all the time."

He let out a short laugh, but then he peered down at her. Ally was proving irresistible to him. Maybe Sutton *had* planned on River falling in love with his assignment. It wasn't a bad plan at all. "What if I want to be your hero?"

Looking into his eyes for a few seconds, she shook her head and pushed herself to her feet. He stood, too, and faced her. He'd kind of assumed that might be a romantic line, but obviously it wasn't, not from the way she was eyeing him like he half-terrified her.

"Maybe I don't want you to be some hero. Maybe I just want you to be River."

He blinked at her. "I don't even know what that means." He couldn't separate himself from that role. He protected. He served. It was who he was.

She folded her arms across her chest and gnawed at her lower lip. The movement of her teeth on her lips distracted River. He forced himself to look into her eyes.

"You." She pushed a hand his direction and shook her head. "You're beautiful and terrifying, and one second I want you to kiss me and the next I want to ... I don't know, hide from how heroic you are, because I'm not heroic, I'm a complete wimp who runs away from my father and ... What?"

River's stomach felt like it was filling up with happy bubbles. It was the oddest sensation. He'd never, ever felt so happy, simply because a woman had said she wanted to kiss him. He couldn't care less if he never worked for Sutton again. Thoughts of anything but Ally were far, far away from this remote place. "You want to kiss me?"

Her lips quirked up in a smile. "That's what you got from all of that?"

He took a step closer and wanted to pump a fist in the air when she didn't back up or look afraid of him. "I got a lot more. We need to work through your emotional junk." He reached up and brushed the hair from her neck.

She shivered and then leaned into his hand. "I'm not the only one with emotional junk," she threw back at him.

"Oh, I know that. Believe me, I know that." He gently pulled her toward him. "And I need to show you that you should never be afraid of me. I would never hurt you."

Ally leaned toward him, and the feel of her body pressed against his sent delicious warmth through him. "I'm not afraid right now."

"Good." He bent down and their breaths intermingled. "And we need to talk about what's going on with your father and work all of that out."

She pulled back slightly, and he knew he should've shut up five seconds ago and just kissed her. "River, my father ... I'll never be free of him."

River wasn't having it. He released her face and wrapped both hands around her lower back, pulling her up and into him. "I'm a hero type, remember? I can save you from anyone."

She shook her head as if she didn't believe him.

River cupped her chin with one hand again. "Do you trust me, Ally?"

She bit at her lip and met his gaze. Her eyes were shining and his heart about burst wanting to rescue her and protect her from every wrong. This was the woman he'd been waiting for. The one he could love and watch over and never grow tired of.

Finally, she nodded.

"I'll protect you," he said in a tone he hoped was reassuring and not demanding.

Ally gnawed at her lip again and then she shook her head. "Just kiss me, River. We can deal with the issues later."

How could she doubt that he could protect her from her father?

But she was right: they could deal with that later. For now, he wasn't going to argue about kissing her.

Ally shoved all the worries about her mum and what her father could do to her, and to River, to the back of her mind as she studied River's handsome face. He slowly leaned closer to her, his large hand cradling her cheek. Last night he'd kissed her, then said he shouldn't have. If he tried that tonight, she'd smack him.

His lips tenderly brushed hers and Ally sighed and melted into him. Tentatively, he met her lips again. She let him take the lead and was shocked by how soft and sweet his kiss was. It was completely different from last night, and though last night's possessive kiss had filled her with warmth and desire, tonight's kiss made her feel cherished and loved.

She pulled back and stared at him. Had she really just thought the word love? Whoa. That was too much, too fast.

River smiled at her and ran his fingers along her neck to cup the back of her head. "You are so beautiful, Ally."

She didn't get a chance to say thank you as he brought her closer and kissed her. He framed her face with his hands and she clung to his biceps, swept away by the joy his kiss brought. His tongue tenderly traced the inside of her lips. Darts of pleasure followed everywhere he touched. She was feeling a bit lightheaded when he finally released her.

"Come on," he said, grinning like a little boy who'd just won the pushcart derby. "We'd better sit and actually keep a lookout."

Pinpricks of fear washed over Ally. She'd forgotten completely about Gray-Face and the possibility that he and an army of hippies could be coming for them.

They got comfortable sitting against her backpack and River took her hand, gently rubbing his thumb against the back of it. She glanced up at him—so strong, so brave, yet so sweet with her. Could he really protect her tonight and in the future? Could anyone protect her from her father's twisted plans and the men he had at his command?

"So, what's going on with your father?" River asked quietly.

Ally shook her head.

He squeezed her hand. "Please let me help you, Ally."

She turned her shoulders so she could stare at him without getting a crick in her neck. "Last night, after you kissed me, you said, 'We can't do this.' Now you want to protect me from my father. Why?"

His eyebrows lifted. "You're direct."

She raised one shoulder but didn't comment.

"I can see that you're terrified of your father, and I don't like bullies. I want to help you."

Ally pulled her hand free and stood. River stood too, his broad chest blocking her path. Ally stepped back and paced in front of him. When she stopped and faced him, a few feet had separated them. She couldn't think clearly with him so close. "Look, I don't expect some lifelong commitment because we shared a few kisses, but you're confusing me. Are you wanting to help me just because of your hero complex, or ..." She couldn't spell it out. If he didn't care for her more than just a fling, she wasn't going to share family secrets with him. She could hire a bodyguard herself. Maybe that was what she should do. Stop trying to run by herself. Hire somebody like River, hire a whole crew who could rescue her mum and protect both of them from her father in some remote African village or someplace like Antarctica where her father wouldn't think to look.

"Ally ..." River pushed a hand through his hair. "I'm confused too, all right? I'm on an assignment, so I shouldn't be getting personally involved, but then there's you—all of you." He gestured with his hand. "It's not just about how beautiful you are. You're also crazy fun and smart and just plain cute and I ... I like being around you, okay? I don't know what that means or what it could develop into, but I know I want to help you and it has nothing to do with my hero complex or getting paid—Ally, get down!"

Ally dropped to the ground, roots and rocks digging into her face, abdomen, and arms. She cried out in pain and fear. She heard a whoosh and a scream. Scurrying on her belly toward River and away from whatever or whoever was behind her, she glanced up as River vaulted over her. Spinning around onto her bum, she squinted into the dark and could see River knock someone to the ground.

Rob, Trevor, and the newlyweds spilled out of their tents. "What happened?" Rob demanded.

"I don't know," she admitted, slowly standing.

"Rob!" River hollered. "Rope!"

Rob and Trevor both nodded and started to hurry away, but Ty held up a hand and stopped them. "I've got rope in my backpack."

Ally's heart beat in her throat, so fast she couldn't catch a breath. What had just happened? Was it Gray-Face or one of the hippies? Were there others around? She strained to hear the sounds of people rushing out of the thick vegetation. Ty pulled the rope out of a backpack, and Rob and Trevor trailed him to River and whoever he was pinning down.

Claire wrapped an arm around Ally. "You okay?"

"Yeah." Ally forced a smile.

They slowly edged their way closer. Ally dwarfed Claire, but she felt reassured with the other woman's arm around her like her mum would've done. As they peered down at the men, it felt like a repeat of last night. Gray-Face was pinned down and River was tying him back up. This time blood was running from a wound on Gray-Face's shoulder and Gray-Face was moaning pitifully. Ally saw River's knife covered with blood next to them on the ground. There was another knife a short distance away. Had Gray-Face had a knife trained on her?

Her stomach rolled and she covered her mouth. River had somehow reacted, yelled for her to get down, and thrown that knife to protect her? She focused on him as he yanked the ropes around Gray-Face's body. He was so much more than his rippling muscles. He truly was her protector. But could she really trust him to protect her from her father? She simply didn't know if one man could take on an army.

CHAPTER FIFTEEN

RIVER HAD SPENT many a miserable night throughout his SEAL training and various deployments, but the hours after he hog-tied Gray-Face again and waited for dawn were pretty awful. None of the group wanted to try to sleep and there was still the worry if the hippies might try and attack as well. They took turns packing up their tents and supplies in the dark, eating and drinking, sometimes talking, but mostly just watching for the sky to lighten so they could get away from Gray-Face and whatever other dangers lay hidden in this beautiful spot.

River felt a sense of responsibility to making sure the authorities arrested the man, but he wasn't willing to hike out of here while dragging Gray-Face's sorry carcass. The loser had lost a significant amount of blood with the knife wound in his shoulder. Unless the hippies cut him loose again, cared for him, and hid him, he wouldn't be going anywhere and should be easy to recapture.

Finally, the sky changed to a deep blue. The group pulled their shoes on their feet and packs on their backs before they could see much more than the next step in front of them. They set out together and River was relieved that they were all in good shape. Ty set a good pace and they pressed on as one, everyone ready to leave the discomfort and fear of Gray-Face miles behind them.

River hardly noticed the majestic beauty of the soaring green peaks and awe-inspiring drops to the ocean far below as the sky lightened. He stayed at the rear of the group and kept checking behind for any sign of someone following them. He did notice Ally walking quietly in front of him. She'd said a lot of things last night that bothered him, but the one that kept ringing through his head was that she was a wimp because she ran from her father. She was so far from a wimp. He couldn't even begin to list all the good things about her, yet he was useless at telling a woman why she was special or amazing. But somehow, someway, he was going to convince her that she was strong and brave, and if he was lucky, she'd let him keep protecting her. Did he dare hope for more?

When he'd seen Gray-Face burst out of the trees behind her last night, with a knife aimed right at Ally, River was lucky he'd been so highly trained. His entire body screamed in horror at the idea of something happening to Ally. He was so glad he'd reacted and yelled for her to drop. Thank heavens she'd listened and he'd been able to nail that loser with his knife. Even now, he felt weak thinking about that guy touching her again.

By late this afternoon they'd be off this trail, get ahold of the police, and then he and Ally were going to shower, order pizza, and talk everything out. Maybe even a little more than talking. He'd forego pizza to kiss her a few more times.

———

Ally's body screamed with exhaustion. Somehow it was even worse than her first trek across this pristine paradise, even though the first time she'd walked an extra seven miles before she started the trail. Maybe it was because the blisters on her heels from the first trek had recently popped and each step hurt. Or maybe it was because she hadn't slept at all the night before. Or maybe it was because all she'd wanted last night after River rescued her from Gray-Face, again, was for him to hold her. He'd watched her carefully like she might break, and he'd been very considerate of her every need, but he hadn't cuddled her into his arms and let her weep with relief that he was here and so strong and brave.

She pushed out a breath. She was a silly girl and River was a trained warrior, a complete stud from head to toe. She didn't deserve him and he didn't need her issues and fears.

They trekked on and the sun came out in full force. The trail was still slick in a lot of spots from the rain the night before last, but nobody complained about the heat or slowed their pace. They made it through Crawler's Ledge and pushed on valiantly. Ally's stomach was rumbling and her legs felt like rubber, but around lunchtime they were at the Hanaka-whatever beach that she couldn't pronounce. They were all smiling and talking more as they realized that they only had two miles left and there were lots of other people at this beach. Safety in numbers really was a true phenomenon. The hippies hadn't followed them or tried to attack them.

As a group, they stopped and shared the snacks they had left in their packs and finished off most of their water, but then they silently pushed on. Ally was carrying River's much lighter backpack, but she was still barely able to put one foot in front of the other as they climbed up the last, mile-long incline. They passed a lot of happy, smiling hikers. It made Ally smile too, but she was so exhausted she could barely mutter a greeting to anyone.

They crested the top of the incline and there were groups of people taking pictures. Ally couldn't resist turning to River with a smile. "Remember when you carried me down this?"

He chuckled, his face relaxing a little bit. It was obvious he'd felt like he needed to protect all of them the past twenty-four hours. "That was a good time. Remember how you kissed me in the waterfall?"

She blushed. "So I'm a bit impetuous."

He grinned. "I like it."

"You two gonna flirt or join us getting down this last mile?" Rob hollered at them.

River chuckled and gestured her in front of him. "Let's go, beautiful lady. I'm ready for some pizza."

Ally smiled and started down the trail. The decline hurt every bit as much as the incline had. Her thighs were screaming for her to stop, but it didn't matter. They were almost there. Pizza sounded good, a shower and a real bed sounded even better, but kissing River sounded like the absolute best.

CHAPTER SIXTEEN

As THEY DESCENDED the last incline to the parking lot, Rob let out a whoop and everyone cheered. People ascending and descending the trail or hanging around by their cars or the showers and bathroom all stopped and stared as they crossed those last few yards. Some of the bystanders started laughing and cheering as well.

The group made it to the flat and River found himself hugging Claire and Ty at the same time, then backslapping Rob and Trevor. They'd survived and accomplished this victory together. He turned to Ally and opened his arms and she flung herself at him. As he held her close, the cheering around him faded away. Nestling her against his chest felt so right.

More people were gawking at or cheering for their little group as Rob thumped River on the back again, interrupting their moment. "Thanks, man. I feel like you saved all of us."

River pulled back from hugging Ally and looked at him. "You did great, bud. I'd take you on my team any day." It was kind of cheesy, but River truly felt a camaraderie with their little group. At the same time he was relieved to be done protecting anyone but Ally. He glanced at her beautiful face. She was smudged with dirt, circles of exhaustion sagged under her bloodshot eyes, and her hair was a ratted mess. She was perfect to him.

He turned to the group. "Thanks, everybody. I really appreciate all of you banding together."

"Thanks for watching out for us," Ty said.

They all hugged one more time, then filtered off to their separate vehicles. River felt a sudden uneasiness with Ally, like a sixteen-year-old at his first formal dance. He had been carrying her larger backpack. He tugged his backpack off her shoulders, savoring the feel of her smooth skin under his fingertips, and murmured, "I better call the police."

She nodded.

Pulling out his phone, he still had no service. "Gonna have to drive until we find service." They walked slowly to the second parking lot where he'd left his Jeep. Climbing silently in, they drove until Ally proclaimed that he had service, and that was all he needed to pull over and call the authorities, explaining everything about Gray-Face and his attacks. He didn't say much about the hippies besides his suspicion that they'd untied Gray-Face. The hippies hadn't really done anything to them, even though he still didn't like those guys or the way they checked out Ally and called her *"pretty girl."*

He kept glancing at Ally. She sat primly with her hands folded in her lap. He wished he could hold her and they could just talk and talk. Soon. That word contented him for the time being. But it had better be very soon.

———

Ally came out of the shower at her rental house and climbed into the soft, cool sheets. River had carried her pack in and told her he'd be back after he showered and got them some food. She was too tired to even eat, and really too tired to hash out with him all of her issues. Maybe he could just hold her while they slept. That sounded perfect. Closing her eyes, she promised herself just a short nap.

The smell of yeasty bread, melted cheese, and spicy pepperoni woke her. Slowly, she opened her eyes to River standing over her bed flapping a pizza box opened and closed. A large grin lit up his handsome face. "Wake up, Sleeping Beauty. I've got two more boxes of pizza, salads, and breadsticks downstairs."

Ally laughed. "You and your pizza! I'll be down in a minute."

"No, come down right now. My mom would skin my hide if I ate without waiting for you, and I am starved." He stood there, waiting, as if to make sure she moved.

"River." She pushed out a breath, her face filling up with heat. "I'm not dressed."

His eyes widened. Slowly, he shut the pizza box and glanced over her form as she lay in the bed. The temperature in the room spiked. "Oh. Um, okay." His mouth was slightly open. "Well, okay, I guess I'll go downstairs then." He clutched the pizza box and hurried to the door, but turned back and said, "Please hurry."

Ally laughed as she scrambled out of bed and slid into a tank top and some yoga pants. After all they'd been through, it was kind of endearing that they'd both been embarrassed about her not being dressed. He'd already seen her in her knickers and various swimming suits, but it felt much too intimate for him to see her like that in her bedroom instead of out on the Nā Pali coastline.

She hurried downstairs, her mouth watering at all the delicious-smelling pizza. Yet the handsome man sitting at her table looked even more scrumptious. He was all freshly washed and wore a simple white T-shirt and gray shorts.

"Would you say a prayer?" River asked quietly.

"Sure." She smiled at him and offered a prayer of gratitude for their safety and a blessing on the food.

"Thanks," he said when she finished. Then he opened a box, grabbed a slice of what looked like meat lover's, and started eating right out of the box.

Ally laughed and followed suit, downing two slices of a barbecue chicken pizza before trying a breadstick. She stood once to get them both glasses of ice water and POGs from the fridge. It all tasted like heaven. Her body was sore and she still felt like she could sleep for a week, but the pizza and being with River made up for all of that.

As she finished her breadstick and a few bites of salad, she sat back and stretched. "I can't eat anymore."

River had eaten a couple of slices of each of the pizzas. He blinked at her. "Are you serious? I don't think I'm going to stop eating all night."

Ally laughed at him. Slowly, she stood and walked to where she had a better view of the beautiful beach. The sun was setting behind the mountains past the beach. Ally appreciated the splendor of it all—the waves rolling in, the verdant peaks, and the sun streaking the low clouds resting on those peaks a lovely pink and orange.

River came up behind her and wrapped his arms around her abdomen. Ally was surprised, but didn't complain as she leaned back into his chest. "It's so beautiful here," she murmured. "I wish I could just stay here forever."

"Open that food truck like Porky's," River said, his breath warm against the side of her face.

"Food van," she corrected.

River laughed. "Let's do it. What kind of food shall we specialize in?"

We. She really liked the sound of *we* coming from his lips. "Fish and chips, of course."

He chuckled. "Sounds good. Maybe we could do some good old American hamburgers and shakes too."

"Perfect." She let the dream linger for a few seconds: her and River, teasing with the locals and the tourists. Working a few hours a day, then hiking or chilling at a beach.

She sighed, reality catching up with her. Her visions of staying here forever were never going to happen. Her father would find her, eventually. And the guilt of knowing what her mum suffered every day was making it heavy for Ally to enjoy the beauty around her, or the beauty of the man with his arms around her. Besides, he was probably just teasing with her. He didn't know her well enough to want to stay with her and protect her.

"Are you ready to tell me about it?" River asked.

Ally pulled away from him and strode back to the table. "You finished, then?"

River nodded shortly, and Ally closed the pizza boxes and started storing them in the fridge. He moved to help her clean up the rubbish.

When they finished, he grabbed a fresh POG for each of them and then took her hand, walking her to the couch. They sat down at the same time—him abruptly, her primly. She could feel his eyes on her, his expectations to know and understand what and who she was afraid of.

"Please talk to me, Ally. I can't help if I don't understand."

Ally turned so she could look at him, pulling her knees up to her chest and wrapping her hands around them so she wouldn't be tempted to grab him and pull him close. "You've already done so much for me, River."

He gave her a soft smile. "We're just getting started."

Ally blinked at him and clung tighter to her legs. She'd never been so tempted to throw herself into someone's arms. His passionate kisses and his tender kisses were both at the forefront of her mind. She'd love to try any kind of kiss with him.

"Are you ready to tell me?" he asked.

Ally leaned back into the cushions and turned her gaze out at the dusky evening. The window was open, so she could hear the waves crashing and—of course—the consistent cockle-doodle-dooing. "I didn't miss the roosters," she murmured.

River laughed. "When we start our food truck and live here, you're going to have to get used to them."

She studied his face. It was possible he was simply teasing her, but it felt deeper, more real than any dream she'd ever had. "Oh, River, I wish that dream could come true."

"Why can't it, Ally? Please tell me."

Ally felt rotten that she was forcing him to drag this out of her. She swallowed and tried to give him a condensed version. "My mum protected me from my father growing up. He didn't care about me one way or another so as long as Mum looked beautiful and appeared at the events that were expected of her. As a child, I assumed she and I had a pretty good life. I knew she was terrified of him, but I don't think it was physical. He's too ... civilized to physically hurt her, and of course he wouldn't want to mess up her perfect face or body."

She swallowed hard, not sure how to explain the depth of her father's emotional abuse. Her father had never touched her, but she and her mum knew the other side of him that no one in public ever saw. He manipulated and twisted the truth until you didn't know much besides the fact that you were worth nothing and he had all power.

She made the mistake of glancing at River and saw the storm brewing in his dark eyes.

"When I graduated secondary school," she continued quickly, "my granddad, my mum's dad, somehow worked it out to get me to America for university. Princeton was ... incredible. I loved my classmates, my school, everything I learned. I know my father was intimidated by my granddad. My father had the title, but he married my mum for the money. He took that money and made it into a fortune with his shipping business, but my granddad still had some control over him. I don't honestly know why my mum didn't turn to Granddad to escape from my father, but she never did. I even caught them fighting about her leaving my father once, and she adamantly refused. The duke has something over her head ... probably me."

Ally sighed, squeezing her legs tighter with her arms. "When I turned eighteen, my granddad transferred most of his fortune into my name. My father was furious, but he couldn't do anything about it." She shuddered. He actually had physically hurt her that day, applying pressure to her hand until she dropped to her knees. She could still see him staring down at her and telling her that he was still in control.

River didn't say anything and it was all spilling out now, so she kept going. "It's hard to explain how it feels. My father belittles and berates until you think you're worth nothing and the fear of crossing him ..." She trembled. His army of "civilized" soldiers could find her anywhere. A few of them had been stationed to watch over her at Princeton in the name of "protection." She knew better. They were there to make sure she stayed in line. "All I ever wanted was to get away. I hate to admit how selfish I was—I guess still am."

River touched her arm. "You're not selfish."

"I am." She swallowed hard. "I should never have left my mum to go to school or to escape here. She helped arrange both things and she loves me so much, but how could I leave her to that ... monster?" Her throat clogged up and tears crested her eyelids. She brushed them angrily away.

River stood and scooped her off the couch. He settled back down with her on his lap and cradled her into his chest. Ally didn't even know how to react, so surprised at his movements, but she craved and loved the comfort and safety of his warm embrace. She released her grip on her legs and snuggled into him. His arms surrounded her and they sat quietly for a few minutes with her simply drawing from his strength.

"Ally?" he whispered roughly.

"Yes?"

"Many men treat women with love and respect. Your father has no right to hurt your mom or threaten you. I promise you I would never hurt you."

Ally listened to his words, soaked them in. She believed him. Her instincts had always told her this about him.

He tilted her chin up and studied her. "How are you so trusting and innocent?"

Ally bit at her cheek. "I'm not really."

"You are. From the first day I met you, I was amazed by your innocence and lack of fear."

"You kind of laughed at my intuition, but I can tell if people have evil intent or not. I knew from the moment I met you that you were good, so it allowed me to be free ... to act like a nutter."

He smiled at her. "You are much too cute." He hugged her closer.

Ally felt so treasured by him, which was silly because they didn't know each other that well.

"So your granddad sort of protected you and your mom, even though he couldn't completely protect you because your mom wouldn't leave your father?"

Ally nodded, hating that they had to get back to this. "My mum doesn't care about the titles, money, or fame, so I have no clue why she wouldn't leave him. I think he threatened her with me, and honestly, the power he has ... It would be impressive if it wasn't so scary." She shook her head. "After I graduated with my master's, I planned to stay in America and work. I loved it so much. People seemed very real to me and I loved the opportunity and freedoms Americans enjoy, but then ... my granddad passed."

River stroked her back with his fingertips. "I'm sorry."

"Thanks." She blinked. As pathetic as she was for falling apart in his arms, she couldn't remember ever feeling this safe. Even with her mum, there was always this underlying current of what her father might do to them. Her mum couldn't really protect her. Not that she was idealistic enough to believe that River could either, but this moment was something she wanted to savor.

They sat quietly for a few minutes and she appreciated that River didn't push her to finish the story, but she wanted to share it with him. "After we lost Granddad I knew I had to go home for my mum. The first few weeks, my father was ... so unlike himself. He was kind and patient with my mum and actually took an interest in me, what I'd studied, what I'd thought of America, what my hopes and dreams were." She let out a harsh laugh and rolled her eyes. "I think most people would've been lured in by it, and I'll admit he's pretty good at his con-artist role, but I always trust my intuition."

"I think your intuition must be pretty amazing if you knew I was a good guy from day one." He winked.

She giggled at that. "That intuition has been good to me." Frowning, she said, "I knew he was up to no good, and when Henry Poppleton started appearing at every dinner and event we went to, I figured it out quick."

"Who's Henry?"

"My ... fiancé."

River started, and Ally was afraid he was going to push her onto the floor. His brows drew together as he stared down at her. "Excuse me?"

Ally laughed. She couldn't help it. The look of bewilderment and despair on his face was endearing and at the same time kind of funny. "I didn't agree to get engaged to him, River. The duke set it all up."

"Okay ..." He slowly settled back into the couch, but he wasn't holding her close anymore.

Ally slid onto the cushion next to him, turning to face him. "I was getting impatient to go start working full-time in America and put into place all the plans I have for using my fortune to help fight human trafficking." Her father treated her and her mum like commodities, so she related more than most to how the victims might feel. She wanted more than anything to help anyone who felt trapped and scared like she did.

River leaned toward her. His eyes filled with interest. "Really?"

"There's this group out of Utah who I've been talking to—Jesse and Cassidy Panetti are my contacts. They have this military guy who they've found recently. He's giving them insight and opportunities to help in different countries than they've been in before ...

What?" She trailed off as he was staring at her like she'd just grown another head.

"How did you meet them?" River asked.

"Through a friend at Princeton. Cassidy's sister-in-law's sister-in-law, if that makes any sense. They keep their group pretty close-knit, so I was lucky that they'd allow me to be involved. Why are you looking at me like I'm wonkers?"

"Nothing. That's an admirable cause." He shook his head and cleared his throat. "But what does that have to do with ... you being engaged?"

"I was making plans to leave home again and my father found out. All of his fake kindness was gone pretty quick. He explained that he'd already set up the announcements for Henry and I's engagement, that Henry would be over that evening to propose and I would say yes. Of course, I told him where he could get off and how fast." She forced a smile, but there was nothing funny about it. "He explained that I had no choice. I could try to run, but he would find me. I could try to tell the media, but they would all take his side, which sadly is true—they all think he's wonderful and think I'm some spoiled, flighty child who deserted them for America. Then he had his body-guards haul me to my room and lock me in there. Told me he'd let me out when I had a change of heart and accepted Henry's ring."

She blew all her air out and chanced a glance at River. He'd folded his brawny arms across his chest and was clutching them so tightly that all the muscles in his biceps, triceps, and shoulders bulged underneath his fitted T-shirt. There was a furrow between his eyebrows.

Ally reached up and rubbed at the furrow. "It's okay, River. I escaped." Her mom had actually drugged the bodyguards while her father was away on business. Maybe River was starting to under-stand how hopeless it was, how her father would catch up with her soon and she wouldn't escape next time.

He grabbed her hand and pulled it against his chest. She could feel his steady heartbeat, and hers sped up with just this simple touch. If her father truly forced her into marrying a spineless bully like Henry, how would she survive? She'd never known such respect and attraction could exist with a man until she'd been around River the past few days.

"I'm going to keep you safe, Ally." The words were comforting, but the sort of growl they escaped with left her feeling a little concerned for anyone who might try to get in River's way. But what was one man against her father's army of cretins?

Still, she smiled at River. What good would it do to tell him how hopeless it was? How she would've already fallen for him if she was free and innocent like he'd thought she was?

"So your mom helped you escape?"

"You keep saying Mom. It's Mum."

He grinned at that. "You're on American soil. It's Mom."

"We'll have to agree to disagree on that one." She looked at their clasped fingers, and she loved the way her hands looked right now. His were strong and tanned and manly, while hers were lean. Her nails weren't their usual manicured white; they were a bit off-color from all the dirt they'd had embedded in them since she'd come to Kauai. If only she could be that girl—carefree and fun, running a food van with the man she loved. A shiver of pleasure darted down her back as she stared into River's dark gaze. She was falling in love with him. No. She couldn't do that. It would make the rest of her life even more miserable. To have loved and lost like her mum had.

She pulled her hand free and stood, going to the open window and listening to the waves and the roosters, staring out at the dark night. Everything was racing through her head—her father's demands; Henry's willingness to comply with anything her father wanted; her mum broken and alone; River so strong and brave, but naïve as to what was going to happen to her.

River rose from the couch and came up next to her. He didn't reach for her, but his simple nearness brought warmth to the pit of her stomach. "You're still afraid," he whispered.

Ally glanced sharply up at him. "You don't know what he's capable of. What he's done to my mum." She shook her head. "It breaks my heart to think of her there, being bullied, belittled, and manipulated by him. A simple word from him and you wish you'd never been born. He'll find me soon and I won't escape again. Soon I'll be just like my mum—broken and miserable."

River spun her to face him, grasping her shoulders between his hands. His face was set in a fierce scowl. "You listen to me. I will never let him hurt you. I will *never* allow you to be broken." His gaze softened as he searched her face, and his scowl dissolved. Then he pulled her in close, wrapped his arms around her back, and simply held her.

Ally allowed herself to relax into his strength. She wrapped her hands around his waist and laid her head on his chest. She loved the impassioned way he'd said that. It was touching and she knew he believed it. Too bad she knew better.

CHAPTER SEVENTEEN

RIVER COULDN'T LET ALLY OUT of his sight. She didn't believe him when he said that he'd protect her, but he could and he would. He'd get Sutton involved. He'd recruit all of his buddies and pay them out of the money he'd been saving to invest into the fight against human trafficking. The Panettis didn't really need his money; they just needed his connections and military experience.

He glanced over at Ally. They were sitting side by side on the couch, holding hands and watching an episode of *Shark Tank*. He'd only seen the show a couple of times, but he could see Ally being on something like that someday. She was beautiful, wise, and wealthy, and she innately wanted to help people. He could see her investing in start-up companies and making people's dreams come true.

How unreal that Ally planned to work with the very people who River trusted more than anyone besides Sutton and his SEAL brothers. He was the military person who was giving them insight into Afghanistan, Iraq, the Philippines, Syria, and Somalia—places he had received extensive training in or him and his buddies had served. It used to be anti-trafficking groups had to search for the hotbeds for trafficking. Now it seemed trafficking was everywhere. Maybe it was just more publicized, but River would fight it as long and hard as he could.

That Ally wanted to help as well just made her even more perfect in his eyes. He was falling for her hard and fast and he knew his buddies would give him grief about how sappy he was feeling, but he didn't care. He'd tell anyone, anywhere, that she was amazing and he'd do anything to keep her close.

Her head slumped to the side, and River had to smile. It'd been a long few days with no rest last night. He picked up the remote and turned off the TV.

Ally straightened. "Sorry. Did I doze off?"

"Only a few times."

"Did I drool too?"

"Yes, ma'am."

She slugged his shoulder.

River laughed. He turned and scooped her off the couch with a hand under her thighs and her back. "Time to sleep, pretty girl." He imitated the hippies' expression for her and started for the stairs.

Ally smiled up at him, but then her grip tightened around his neck. "Can you stay here?"

He glanced down at her, hating that her blue eyes were filled with fear again. "You just try and kick me out," he teased.

She relaxed a little bit, her smile growing. "But don't get any ideas. I'm a good girl."

River carried her up the stairs. "Says you."

"Oh!" Ally protested, trying to squirm from his arms.

River held her tight against his chest, chuckling at her protest. He walked into her bedroom and stopped next to the bed, still holding her tight. She stopped struggling and stared up at him, all wide-eyed and beautiful.

"You are a good girl, Ally," he whispered. He lowered his head and she arched up, meeting him halfway. The kiss was pure and innocent. River's heart was thumping and he wanted more from her, much more, but he was willing to take it slow and do this right.

Gently, he laid her on the bed. She stretched out and smiled. "Ah, that feels nice."

River couldn't believe how good she looked to him. Miles past "nice," at least. Staying here might not be a good idea. He took a step back. "I'll, um, sleep in the next room. Good night." He turned and would've walked away.

"River, please." The slight tremble in her voice stopped him cold. "I need you close."

River turned and he could feel his chest expanding and contracting quickly, the heat pulsing through his body. She was too good, too beautiful, too innocent. She *needed* him. He didn't know that he was strong enough to stay close and yet stay far away.

———

Ally was playing with fire and she knew it, but with River by her side there was hope. Maybe he really was as strong and brave as he looked. Maybe he really could take her father's bullies to task and come out the victor. But it was much more than just the need to feel safe and comfortable. It was River. She was falling in love with every burly inch of him. He treated her so tenderly yet could still make her smile and laugh. He told her that she was cute, and she loved that it wasn't just some physical thing; he thought she was fun and adventuresome. He could keep up with her and challenge her and he was good through and through. She needed him and she wanted him and the thought of being separated from him, even by a thin wall, was too much.

River walked so slowly and carefully back to her that she couldn't even hear his footfalls over the steady thrumming of her heart. He stopped next to the bed and gazed down at her. His eyes stayed focused on her face, but the heat in his gaze could've set a green willow branch on fire.

"I don't know if I'm strong enough to stay in here," he murmured.

The words rumbled through her as delicious as the heat in his gaze, but they were almost scarier than being left alone. "You're stronger than any man I've ever met."

His gaze swept over her and he swallowed hard. "You have no clue what you do to me, Ally."

She smiled and soaked in this feeling for a minute—being desired by a man who was more heroic and desirable to her than any man she'd ever met.

He pushed out a breath and then raked his fingers through his hair. "You're laughing at me."

"Never. I love that you feel the same way I do."

Time stretched between them as he looked at her, deeper than anyone ever had before. His eyes traveled down her body and back up. "Get in the covers."

Ally blinked in surprise. He wouldn't take advantage of her; she knew that. Maybe he'd misunderstood what she meant by needing him.

His expression softened. "You sleep under the covers and I'll find a blanket and sleep on top of the covers."

Relief whooshed through her. This man. She'd never been so captivated by anyone. She scrambled under the covers. River bent down and carefully tucked the covers under her sides and her chin. She felt like a little child swaddled and cared for.

He smiled at her. "Don't ... move."

Ally laughed. "Blimey, I wouldn't dare. Sir, yes sir!" She would've saluted, but she couldn't get her hand free.

River chuckled, shaking his head at her.

"There's an extra blanket in the closet," she told him.

He grabbed the blanket, flipped off the light, and settled on the other side of the bed. The bed was too big and he felt much too far away. Ally thought back to sleeping in that cramped tent with him. Now *that* had been a good sleeping arrangement. She bit at her lip and commanded herself to stop all these wanton thoughts. She was saving herself for marriage. A dark image sprang into her brain. *Please not a marriage to Henry.*

River's breaths were shallow and she could hear them over the roosters crowing and the waves rolling onto the shore.

"Do you wonder if the roosters ever shut up?" Ally asked.

River laughed. "You're the one who wants to live here permanently."

Ally sighed. She almost wished they didn't have this dream together. It would make life so much harder when her father did find her and awful reality slammed her back to the hard, cold earth.

"You don't really believe it will happen," River muttered. "You don't really believe I can protect you."

It wasn't a question, but Ally answered him anyway. "You're stronger than any man I know and I've seen a bit of your fighting and security skills." Ally sighed. "Thank you for being the hero, River, but I don't think you understand. When my father finds me, he'll send an army."

River moved quickly. One second he was too far away, and the next his chest was pressed against her arm and his face was so close she could see his deep brown eyes, even in the dark room. He smelled clean and delicious. "I have an army of my own, Ally."

Ally stared up at him, her heart threatening to burst. She couldn't pull her arms free to hug him tight and she couldn't move enough to kiss him, and the words bubbling up from her soul were too quick and absolutely insane, but she said them anyway. "I think ... I fancy you, River."

River smiled and whispered, "I more than fancy you, Ally."

He lowered his head and their lips connected. Ally's heart was beating out of control and every nerve in her mouth sung in response to River's warm lips and his sweet words. His lips caressed hers so tenderly, and then he increased the pressure, taking control like the warrior he was. When he deepened the kiss, she felt like she was soaring. There was no thinking about it. She loved him and he loved her back. Who cared if her father found her and ripped them apart tomorrow? Tonight she was with River, and that was more than enough.

CHAPTER EIGHTEEN

RIVER'S EYES WERE HEAVY. He didn't want to open them, but he had to. Something was wrong. He had to protect Ally. Forcing his eyes open, he glanced around at the still-dark room. He'd fallen asleep with Ally still nestled under the covers. One of his hands was resting on the pillow, entangled in her silky hair; the other arm had been draped protectively across her abdomen.

What had woken him? He strained but heard nothing. Closing his eyes, he started to drift off when he heard it again. Movement. Someone was in the house.

He scrambled off of the bed and to his feet. His weapons were downstairs in his backpack. How could he have been so careless? He bent down and shook her. "Ally," he whispered harshly.

She opened her eyes sleepily. "Ri—"

He clapped his hand over her mouth to silence her, and her eyes widened. "Someone's here," he whispered. "Get in the bathroom. Lock the door. Call the police." He grabbed her cell phone off the nightstand and shoved it at her.

She grasped the cell phone and scrambled out of bed.

Ripping the curtain rod off the wall, he dropped the curtain and crept over to stand next to the open bedroom door. Whoever came through wasn't going to like what they got.

Ally gave him a look of fear and desperation as she quietly shut the bathroom door. He heard the lock click, but the knowledge that she was behind a locked door was only a small reassurance. There were glass doors running the length of the master suite's patio, and one of them led into the bathroom. He hated the thought of someone climbing up to the patio and breaking through that door to Ally, but the movement was coming from the stairs. He had no clue who was here or what he was facing, but he'd protect Ally and she'd get the police coming. It'd be fine. Everything would be fine.

The muffled steps stopped in the hallway. Whoever it was, they were stealthy. River's stomach swooped with anticipation when the first man cleared the door; he could see the person was in full battle gear, complete with infrared goggles. All of Ally's fears of her father sending an army rushed through his mind as he swung the wooden curtain rod like a battle axe.

The man didn't shout, but River could hear the air whoosh out of him on impact as his body folded around the curtain rod. He was thrown back into the man behind him. River heard grunts of surprise and could almost feel the rush of manpower in the hallway. He wouldn't mind fighting anyone who dared come after Ally, but he couldn't risk one getting past him to her. He made a command decision and swung the door back closed, throwing his body weight against it.

He wanted to scream for Ally to call the police, but she was smart and he'd rather not alert whoever was out there that help was coming. It was enough they knew they were meeting resistance. How many were there? He could take on the British Army if it meant protecting Ally, but he really wished he had his weapons.

The door vibrated against his back. The men in the hallway didn't say a word as they threw themselves at the door to try to bust it open. River was surprised they hadn't shot at the door, but if they really were her father's men, they'd probably been instructed to not shoot and possibly harm her.

Closing his eyes, he strained against the door, his thighs burning, but he felt optimistic. Ally was safe, surely she'd called the police, and if these men didn't use gun power, they wouldn't get through this door, or River, before help arrived.

His eyes popped open as the resistance on the other side stopped. There was no way they'd given up. He glanced out at the patio that ran the length of the master suite. Please, no. Several men jumped over the ledge, and then he heard Ally scream.

"No!" River pushed off of the door and leapt at the locked bathroom door, knocking it open on his first try with the weight of his body. He crashed to the slate floor. Glass shattered and the glass door that led into the bathroom from the patio crumbled to the deck.

Ally ran toward him from across the large bathroom. River scrambled to his feet. Two men in black seized Ally by the arms before he could reach her, lifting her off her feet.

"Ally!" he hollered as he rushed toward her.

Someone tackled him from behind. Glass sliced into his face and arms. He bucked the man off, but three more took his place. Before he could do much more than throw an elbow back into one man's face, River was shoved to the bottom of a scrum far worse than any football pileup to retrieve a fumble.

River kicked out and felt a nose give way under his bare foot. With his one free hand, he grabbed a man under his goggles and shoved his head through the vanity cupboard. As he kicked another man, two of them jumped on his arm, immobilizing it. River wrenched his other arm free and wrapped it around one of their necks. With this leverage he couldn't break a neck, but it only took six seconds to choke a man out.

He felt a needle jam into the immobilized arm and cool liquid enter his bloodstream. River bucked his body and yanked his arm back, but there were too many bodies on top of him. He could hear Ally calling for him over the murmur of quiet grunts and commands.

"Ally!" he screamed out one more time. Then everything went dark.

CHAPTER NINETEEN

"RIVER! RIVER!" Ally screamed his name over and over again. He'd been fighting valiantly, but then he disappeared beneath at least a dozen black-clad bodies. Two men restrained her as she fought to get free and get to River. What would they do to him? "No! Stop!"

A man strode toward her and pulled a needle out.

"No!" Ally flung her body the other direction to try to escape him.

The two men holding her were each almost as large as River, and as one they pushed her against the bathroom wall, lifting her off her feet and holding her completely still. Ally kicked her feet and swung her head, but that was all she could move.

Her heart was beating so hard she couldn't catch a breath. Cold terror sliced through her as the man with the needle approached. He didn't look malevolent, just businesslike as he pushed his body against her right leg, then plunged the needle into her thigh.

"River!" She looked desperately at the pile on the floor, feeling the icy medicine enter her leg. The men on the pile helped each other up, and River's body came into view. He lay motionless, along with at least four of his attackers, but she didn't care about them.

River's face was relaxed, tilted to the side with his eyes closed. No! They'd killed him. Pain crashed into her that had nothing to do with her physical body. River. Oh, River. He'd died protecting her.

"River," she moaned, feeling the fight leaking out of her, replaced by pain and haze. Without River, nothing mattered.

Her tongue felt thick and her vision darkened. She could feel her pulse thumping with fear, but her head seemed to be swelling. Thick blackness surrounded her, dragging her down into an endless sea of nothingness.

CHAPTER TWENTY

ALLY WOKE with a splitting headache and the smell of sweet vanilla filling her senses. "Mum," she croaked out, turning her head on the feather pillow, but unable to open her eyes. It just hurt too much.

"Oh, sweetheart." Her mum bent down and held her close.

Ally breathed in the familiar vanilla aroma and took a small amount of comfort in her mum's embrace, but then it all came rushing back. There was no comfort, protection, or happiness for her anymore. "River?" she croaked out.

She could feel her mum's head shaking back and forth. "I'm so sorry, sweetheart."

"He killed him, didn't he?"

"I'm so sorry."

Ally's heart felt like it was being wrenched from her body. She'd known her father was a monster and that he'd ruin her life, but to take River's life? Tears burned as they slid out of her closed eyes. She couldn't open her eyes and face a world where River was gone.

A lock clicked, and the door to her bedroom opened and closed. Sharp taps announced the duke striding toward her bedside. She could smell his Clive Christian cologne. The citrus and jasmine combination made her gag. She wanted to jump up and gouge his eyes out, but her body was weak and her stomach was churning and the best she could do was turn her head away and refuse to acknowledge him.

"Good morning, my darlings." His voice boomed throughout the room. "Is my pumpkin feeling better?"

She could hear her mum standing to face him. "You need to leave—" she said in a low tone, only to break off with a cry as she hit the floor with a sickening thud.

Ally sat up and her head threatened to split in two as she screamed, "Stop! No!" She didn't think her father had physically hurt her mum before, but now she realized she'd been stupid and innocent and her mum had lied to her to protect her. River had been spot-on when he'd first met her. She was a spoiled brat who didn't have a clue.

Her father looked up at her with a placating smile as he pushed her mum's face into the marble floor. Luckily she couldn't see any blood and her mum's eyes were blinking.

Ally clutched her own head. "Stop! Stop, you evil maggot!" It sounded like the useless insult of a little girl, and she hated herself for it.

Her father's smile widened. "You actually cared for that lousy excuse of a bodyguard, did you?"

Ally glared at him, refusing to give him the satisfaction.

"He's dead now." He paused to let it sink in, and it was all Ally could do to not sob. "If you want someone else you love to die, keep up the pouty attitude." He released her mum suddenly and yanked her up to her feet. Her mum swayed but looked all right, besides the terror in her eyes. "If you want everybody to stay happy and alive, I suggest you say yes to Henry when he comes to visit tonight." He patted her mum's cheek condescendingly. "I've been considering upgrading to a newer model anyway." With a sneer, he shoved her back into the chair by the side of the bed and strode from the room. The lock clicked back into place from the outside. He must've had the lock reversed.

Ally lay back onto the pillows and didn't even try to stop the tears streaking down her face. He would kill her mum. She didn't doubt it for one second.

"Now you listen to me." Her mum pressed her lips right up next to Ally's ear. "We'll toe his line for now, but we are getting out of here."

"What's the use?" Ally muttered. He'd taken River. What else did she have to live for besides her mum? She couldn't trade her mum's life for freedom, temporary as the freedom would be.

"I will not allow you to live the life I've lived. I won't."

Ally turned her head and looked at her mum's picture-perfect face. She'd heard many times that her mum was the most beautiful woman in the world. The people who said that must never have looked into her eyes, never seen the pain.

Ally threw her arms around her mum's neck. Her mum hugged her back. "I love you," Ally whispered. "But you are completely delusional."

"I love you," her mom whispered back. "And I'll die before I let you submit to him."

CHAPTER TWENTY-ONE

RIVER'S HEAD was splitting in two. Bright sunlight tried to poke through his eyelids, but he kept them screwed shut. His arms and legs were heavy and almost unresponsive, and that scared him enough to force his eyes open. Several young men gazed down at him, but he couldn't make out much more than that they were skinny and didn't smell great. The sun was just too bright. Where was Ally? It was all so fuzzy right now. The men in black breaking through the glass door. The fight, the needle, Ally screaming for him. Too many, there were just too many. He'd told her he could protect her, and he'd failed.

"He's alive," one of the young men called out.

River heard some cheering, which made his head hurt worse. His stomach rolled. "Where am I?" he forced out.

"Hanalei Bay."

That made sense. He could feel the sand underneath him, the waves crashing and lapping against the beach. The stupid roosters. Thinking of the roosters reminded him of Ally again. Where had they taken her? Back to England? Was she hurting, scared, alone? He couldn't stand to think of them hurting her.

"Why do you look familiar?" he muttered at the young men, his eyes gradually adjusting to the sunlight and their faces coming into focus.

"Dude! You're the reason we got kicked out of Kalalau. The rangers came in with pepper spray and everything."

River's head was threatening to burst and he was going to puke soon. He had no clue what this kid with blond dreadlocks was telling him. "I'm ... sorry."

"It's chill." The kid did the hang-loose sign. "Sorry we cut that creeper free and he almost hurt your girl. He was bad news. We left him tied up the second time, but the rangers still ripped us a new one. Where's the pretty girl?"

"Ally." Her name tore from his chest in a sort of moan. "They took her."

"Okay, chill, military man. You've got to get feeling better and then you can go bust some heads and save the day. Try this. Willow bark. It helps after a hangover."

"I'm not hungover," River protested, but he sank back onto the sand and chewed whatever bitter herb the kid handed to him. He didn't know if he could save the day. Where had they taken Ally?

He looked back at the kid, grateful they all had at least swim trunks on now. "You just found me here on the sand?" Why would the duke's men have moved him, and why did he feel so waterlogged?

"Naw, man, you were half in the ocean. Someone tossed your body in there last night, probably thinking you'd drown and the police would think you were just another idiot who got drunk and tried to swim at night. But we saw you early this morning and went after you, bro."

Was River's brain just scrambled, or had his enemies become his friends? "Thanks. You saved my life."

Dreadlocks grinned. "We're not doing some blood oath where you have to follow me around until you save my life too, right?"

River couldn't help but laugh, which hurt. "Under normal circumstances, yes, but I've got to go find Ally."

"Whew. Good. No offense, military man, but I think you'd cramp-a my style."

River smiled, certain that was the truth. The kid offered him a water bottle and he lifted his head enough to guzzle half of it down.

The nasty herb actually seemed to be working as his head wasn't hurting quite as much. Ally had been right. He should've listened to her and taken better precautions and gotten her to Sutton immediately. Who knew the duke could find them so quickly? It wasn't time for regrets, but he could still hear Ally screaming for him in that bathroom as he'd fought and suffocated underneath the pile of men. He'd claimed he could protect her and he'd failed.

A plan started to form in his mind. He'd need Sutton and his SEAL buddies, but he'd also need to turn to the one person he'd stopped turning to years ago. He looked at the kid. "Do any of you have a phone I can borrow?"

"Sure, military man. Just take it easy, though. You're pretty thrashed, you know?"

"Thanks, but I really need a phone."

"Okay." Dreadlocks stood and went to his group of friends, who'd congregated around a pavilion of sorts.

River lay back in the sand until Dreadlocks came back with the phone in hand. "Unlimited minutes, too." The kid grinned like he had a million bucks.

"I'll pay you back," River grunted.

"Hey, none of that. We told you already we don't want your stinking money."

River clasped the hand the kid held out to him and let him help him into a seated position. "You're a good guy," River said. "What's your name, man?"

"Quinn."

"Nice to meet you. I'm River."

Quinn nodded. "Good luck saving the pretty girl. I'll be over there if you need anything." He pointed at the pavilion.

"Thanks."

River had to close his eyes and think. He was good with numbers, but he had them all plugged into his phone and didn't usually have to think about it. Besides, everything in his head was still a little scrambled.

After two wrong tries, he finally heard the voice he wanted. "Smith."

River felt a rush of gratitude that left him feeling even weaker. "Sutton, it's River. I need ... a lot of help."

"Name it."

River smiled and squeezed his eyes shut. He laid his ideas out to Sutton, and of course Sutton improved upon it. Was his brain completely muddled, or did Sutton sound excited about the plan? Within a few minutes, River was repeating "heart of a warrior," hanging up the phone, and dialing again.

This time the number was embedded in his memory. His hand shook slightly. Would his father be willing to help him? River knew the barrier between them was built from both sides, but he also knew his father did care for him, in his own way.

"Hello?" The voice was cautious.

"Mom?" he croaked out.

"Channing? Are you okay, sweet boy? You don't sound okay. Where are you calling from?"

"I'm fine, Mom." Though he was so far from fine it wasn't even funny, and hearing his mom's voice made him want to go home and have her give him a hug, tell him he was handsome, and put a cool cloth on his head. "Is Dad there?" Sutton had said it was Sunday, so his dad might be home.

"Channing ..." Her voice lowered. "What is going on?"

"I need Dad." The words tasted bitter. He'd needed his father many times throughout his life and had always been let down when work had come first.

"You haven't asked for your daddy in ... well, you never have."

River couldn't help but grin at that. "I'm sorry, Mom. I love you and you know you're my favorite, but I need Dad right now."

"Barry?" his mom screeched not far from the phone, and River winced. Then he could hear his mom moving and pulling in quick breaths. "Barry, it's Channing. He wants to talk to you!"

River felt emotion bubbling in his chest. This was not the time for that. He could barely hold his head up, and he had to rescue Ally.

"Channing?" His dad's voice was cautious.

"Dad." The word rushed out and it was too full of emotion. He was too old and removed from family to be feeling this needy, but he knew his dad wasn't the enemy. He was a workaholic and they didn't see eye to eye, but his dad still loved him and he was pretty sure he'd help him. "Dad," he began. "I'm sorry, and I ..." Man, this was as tough as he'd always imagined it would be. "I need your help," he forced out.

His dad pulled in a breath, then said, "Anything, Channing. I'd do anything to help you."

River blinked hard. He couldn't form words, but he knew his dad was telling the truth.

CHAPTER TWENTY-TWO

ALLY ENTERED the stately ballroom on Henry's arm. She loathed touching him. Her mum and father were just ahead of her, looking regal and picture-perfect in a black tux and silver formal. This was Lord Kingsley's party, the fourth party she'd attended this week as an engaged woman. She hated each party more than the last. Dressing in formals with the maids fixing her hair and makeup to perfection. People she'd known for years or hardly knew at all gushing over the size of her diamond, how lucky she was to marry Henry Poppleton, how she looked just like her mum. She endured it all with a fake smile on her face. Did they have any clue she was as miserable as her mum as well? At least she knew that Lord Kingsley and his son, Blake, loathed Henry. It was a small comfort, because Lord Kingsley was in the House of Lords with her father so he was no help to her, but it made her like them more that they despised Henry like she did.

Her mum kept reassuring her they would find a way to escape, but as each day went by Ally grew more and more despondent. River was gone. She couldn't think about him without sobbing, so she only let herself think about him late at night, alone in her room.

She'd loved him before, but now, knowing that he was gone, it was a desperate love that she didn't think she'd ever get over. He'd given his life for her, and for what? So she could be as wretched as her mum had been?

Now her father had complete control. She knew it was all a money-and-power game for him, plus he was the spawn of Satan, but she wouldn't allow him to kill her mum and she didn't doubt he'd do it if she crossed him. That comment about *upgrading* kept ringing through her head, and making her ill every time. If she and her mum escaped together that was the only way she'd go, but she doubted very much it was possible.

Cameras flashed around her and Henry pulled her tight against his side, his hand moving over her bare back. She would've loved the white dress with the form-fitted bodice, embroidered flowers, and full skirt, if she wouldn't have been next to Henry in it. He kissed her cheek, murmuring, "You look gorgeous, Alexandria."

She grinned for the cameras. "You're a weasel," she whispered back.

Henry ignored her. He knew exactly what she thought of him, but he and her father had made a financial deal and all he cared about was that his bride had the right bloodlines and looked like a model on his arm.

She'd tried to talk to him the first time they were alone and tell him exactly what her father was like and beg him to help her and her mum. She could still remember his condescending look and his words: "Your father told me you'd be a perfect wife for me or you'd suffer a penalty that the two of you had arranged. Do you need me to relay this information to him?" She'd quickly given him an unequivocal and hopefully convincing no. For the first couple of days, she had tried to act perfect. Then she'd figured out she could make snide comments and he wouldn't react. It made her feel a little better.

Her father and Henry hadn't stopped talking on the drive over about the American billionaire who was going to be at this party tonight—Barry Duncan. Their words washed over Ally because she didn't care, but apparently the man had contacted her father to make sure he'd be at this party. He wanted to see about transferring his international shipping needs to her father's company.

Barry Duncan. Ally was certain she'd hate him as much as any other wealthy man, but just hearing an American would be there gave her a twinge of hope. Which was insane. But maybe, just maybe, she could get a dance with this Barry. And maybe, just maybe, she could confide in him what was going on with her and her mum and he would contact River's friend, Sutton Smith. She was nuts to even hope, especially if the man was a business associate of her father's, but the wheels still spun and no matter how she ached for River and despaired of ever being free, she could never fully give up on at least protecting her mum.

"There are a lot of media here tonight," Henry remarked.

Ally nodded, glancing around. The ballroom could hold hundreds of people, and tonight proved it. She recognized most of the faces as England's wealthy and titled, but there were quite a few men she didn't know mingling amongst the throng—well-built men who reminded her of River. Would she ever stop thinking about him?

Servers circled with drinks and refreshments. More cameras flashed at Ally and Henry. She hoped the loathing she felt for him didn't show on her face. Controlling herself protected her mum from being hurt, or worse. Looking around, her heart sank—she'd lost track of her mum in the crush of people.

Couples were dancing, but luckily Henry wasn't much for dancing. He escorted her to a spot where they'd get a lot of attention and pictures; then he started chatting with a group of his business associates. He'd used his family money to build up box stores throughout Europe, which was why her father wanted the union. It would secure his shipping companies billions of dollars in revenue.

Ally took a glass of champagne and toyed with it, remembering how River almost refused her sleeping-potion-filled piña colada because he thought it had alcohol in it. She smiled to herself. He'd been so great about her knocking him out and escaping. Then he'd come after her and protected her from Gray-Face. She let herself think about that night in the tent. His grin. His kisses. A tear crested her eyelid and she discreetly wiped it away, but then they started coming faster and she couldn't stop the flow.

"Excuse me," she said to the group. "I think I'm allergic to something." She blinked quickly and sniffled.

"Run quickly before your makeup smears," a lady on her right said.

Yeah, that was what she was worried about.

Henry nodded his encouragement and she walked swiftly away. Grateful for the reprieve, she hid behind some huge potted plants, set her untouched champagne glass on the floor, and simply watched the people, letting the tears flow as she thought of River.

Her mum danced past her, in the arms of a handsome and dapper-looking gentleman with short, dark hair, and a tall stature that just looked impressive, like he was no one to toy with. Her mum looked uncomfortable yet all lit up at the same time. That look in her eyes was one Ally had never seen before, so she studied the gentleman again.

Ally's mouth fell open. Was that the American businessman? Did her mum know him? They had a familiar manner, and the way the man was gazing at her mum made Ally feel like she'd intruded on a lover's tryst.

She glanced around the room and saw her father in conversation with a broad man. Every few seconds her father's gaze would dart to her mum, and a look of sheer fury would flit across his brow before he'd refocus on the man next to him. Ally watched the man next to her father, and he caught her gaze and smiled briefly before looking back at her father. He resembled River, she thought. Same indentation in his cheek when he smiled, same deep brown eyes. *Oh my goodness.* Every man couldn't remind her of the one she'd lost.

More tears surfaced. She probably should find the loo. She was a mess. Instead of finding the loo, she shrank deeper into the shelter of the huge potted plants.

"Oh, Ally, I've missed you," a deep voice murmured in her ear.

Ally's stomach swooped and her heartbeat picked up. It couldn't be, could it? She whirled to face the man.

River stood close by, devastatingly handsome in a tailored navy-blue tuxedo. His dark eyes twinkled at her. "Hello beautiful," he said.

"River, but … they killed you." It was too much. The whole room swam and it all pressed on her like a heavy waterfall. Her knees gave out and she sank toward the ground as everything went black.

———

"Ally!" River grabbed her as she passed out, catching her before her head hit the ground. Her father had told her he was dead? Of course, the duke assumed they'd killed him, but somehow River had fooled himself into believing Ally would know how tough he was, that he couldn't be killed that easily. His stomach tightened at the thought of her suffering this past week.

Ally's eyes fluttered open and she stared up at him. "River, oh, River." Then she was sobbing in his arms, and he cradled her close and let her cry.

Slowly, he pulled her farther back into the potted plants. He'd been lucky that she'd gotten away from her fiancé, and his father was doing a great job keeping the duke captivated with some business proposal that would never come to fruition. Sutton had surprised him, dancing around with Ally's mom like he was smitten with her. He didn't figure Sutton for the dancing type, and *never* for the romantic type, but it was a fabulous way to distract Ally's father. Sutton really was a James Bond.

River glanced down at Ally. It had been the longest week of his life, getting everything in place when all he wanted to do was swoop in and rescue her, kicking a lot of butts in the process. "Love," he whispered in her ear. "I'm so sorry you thought I was dead."

She looked up at him, so trusting and filled with love. "I was so gutted. And now you're here, you beautiful, splendid stud of a man." Tears squeezed past her long lashes. "You're really here."

He grinned, but then sobered quickly. "I'm sorry I underestimated the duke, but my army is mobilized for war now. Are you ready to be rescued?"

She clung to him. "Oh, River, it's hopeless. He'll kill my mum like he claimed he killed you. He'll really do it."

River stole a quick kiss, wanting much, much more but contenting himself with knowing very soon he'd have her all to himself. He stood and pulled her up to her feet next to him. "I've got a plan that will protect you and your mom, but you've got to play your part. Can you do that?" He hated to push her when she was obviously a mess thinking he was dead and brought back to life and so worried about her mom. But this was his best opportunity to get her away from her father and that weasely-looking guy she'd come in with.

Ally wiped at her eyes and straightened her hair, resolve shining in her bright blue gaze. "Of course I can. What do you think I've been doing my whole life?"

He chuckled. "That's my girl. Now, before we go out and make a scene, I have to know the answer to one question. Will you marry me?"

———

Ally's head spun, threatening to make her pass out again. "Wh-what?"

River held her tenderly, staring down at her. He was so perfect. He was alive. She'd do whatever he wanted, but was he only asking because he wanted to be the hero? "Will you marry me?" he repeated.

"River." She ran her hands up his arms, feeling the solid muscle there, the comfort and excitement of him. Cupping his exquisite face with her hands, she said, "Are you asking because of your hero complex and you need somebody to protect, or because you really love me?"

He grinned, and that slight indentation in his left cheek made her knees go weak. "I like being your hero," he admitted, "but I fancy you, Ally. I've fallen in love with you. This past week without you has been torture. Please marry me, and we'll go fight human trafficking together and open a fish-and-chips food truck on Kauai in our spare time."

"Yes," Ally said. "Blimey, yes, I want to save children and run that food van with you."

River chuckled.

Ally's heels gave her a little more height, but she still had to lift up to kiss him. River's lips met hers and an explosion of happiness crackled around them. He held her tight to his body and she wanted nothing more than to escape with him.

He released her after much too short of a kiss and encircled her waist with his hand. "Okay, it's show time, love. Just follow my lead."

Ally swallowed and gave him a brave smile. "I'd follow you anywhere."

"Now that's not true. I'm the one always following you."

She smiled, and it was genuine. River was here. She didn't care about anything else. He was alive and more perfect than she remembered, and she hardly felt afraid of how her father would react when he saw them together.

River escorted her out to the middle of the room, and Ally searched for her mum and found her next to her father again. She gave Ally an encouraging smile and a nod, but fear traced an icy finger up Ally's spine. Her mum. Ally couldn't marry River without her father taking it out on her mum once they were alone. What about his threat of upgrading? Ally wouldn't put anything past him.

How could her mum be so relaxed and confident? Could River really protect them both?

"My mum," she whispered urgently in River's ear. It seemed like the entire room had stopped talking and was staring at them. She noticed the music had stopped also.

River bent close to her. "See the people next to your father?" She followed his gaze and noticed the same burly man who'd been talking to the duke earlier, alongside a short, adorable-looking lady with dark curls springing out of her head and a wide smile on her lovely face.

"Those are my parents. My dad's going to distract your father and my mom and Sutton will rescue your mom."

Ally went all gooey inside. They hadn't known each other very long, but River knew exactly what she needed—her mum to be safe. "You're in England now. It's mum."

River threw back his head and laughed. Then he leaned close and gave her a lingering kiss. "I love you."

Ally's whole body warmed, like she'd been lit up from the inside.

"What is going on here?" Henry popped up front of them.

River's eyes traveled up and down Henry and flashed him a dismissive, insincere smile. Then he reached for Ally's left hand and gently slid the five-carat diamond off. Ally felt the relief of the massive, gaudy ring leaving her finger, and without its weight she felt as if she could float.

River tossed the ring to Henry, who caught it automatically. "Excuse us, please," River said cordially.

"I will not excuse ..." Henry started, but he trailed off as four buff dudes in tailored suits surrounded him.

Mischief sparked in the rebel-looking one's eyes as he gave Alexandria an up and down. "Good for you, River," he teased.

One who looked like Thor elbowed Corbin. "Dude, stop." He winked at River. "Heart of a Warrior."

River let out a light laugh. "Heart of a Warrior," he repeated.

The men escorted Henry toward the side of the room.

"You know those guys?" Ally whispered.

"That's part of my army." River winked. "Navy, actually, but we're amphibious."

Ally laughed. She saw some more of the well-built men she'd noticed earlier in the night had her father's lackeys cornered. Her hopes lifted.

Lord Kingsley strode toward them with a preacher at his side. The preacher didn't look like any vicar she'd ever met. He had emerald-green eyes, brown hair, a military haircut, and a life-is-good smile on his face.

"River," the vicar greeted them. "And the lovely Alexandria."

"Cannon." River gave him a fist-bump. "Eyes off my girl."

Lord Kingsley pumped his eyebrows at Ally, then turned to the crowd. "We have a most unusual turn of events for our party this evening," he said in his booming voice. "My dear friend's daughter, Alexandria Gunthry, is going to be married. You'll have to forgive her for marrying an American." He threw back his head and roared with laughter. The crowd joined in, though their laughter was more perfunctory. "Who can argue with young love? Well, Vicar, take it away."

Ally couldn't help but glance at her parents. Her father's features were like stone with a fake smile carved onto his face. Her mum had tears running down her cheeks, and she nodded to Ally.

River took both of her hands in his and she turned to face him. "Sorry it's a bit untraditional, love."

"I don't care. I'll be with you."

He squeezed her hands and the vicar started right into their vows, which she was so grateful for as cameras flashed around them. All she wanted was to be married to River and escape somewhere with him. Somewhere far from the duke. Would he really leave her alone if she was married to River? Would this Sutton guy really be able to rescue her mum?

Ally said "I do" at the right time and listened as River said it as well, but she was lost in his dark gaze. When he slid an exquisite two-carat round diamond with a thick gold band on her finger, she loved the rightness of the ring. She slid the simple gold band that River handed her onto his finger. He grinned at her, and the depth of this moment hit her. They were married. It was insane and too quick, but instead of feeling weighed down and terrified like she had felt with Henry, she felt light, airy, safe, and so in love.

River leaned in to seal their vows with a kiss, and the worries over her mum and the fear and misery of the past week disappeared. His lips were warm and he took command of her world. The crowd cheered as the newlyweds parted and turned to face them.

People rushed in to offer their congratulations, and it was all a blur of happy wishes and the rush and joy of being married to River. Crazy, happy joy ... until they got to her parents. Her father gave her a perfunctory hug and whispered harshly in her ear, "A simple battle doesn't win the war, pumpkin."

Ally yanked away from him, fear coursing through her as she saw the familiar daggers in her father's eyes. The war was far from over, but River took her hand in his, reminding her the duke couldn't hurt her with River close by. Yet the memory of River being tackled by her father's men in that bathroom in Kauai surfaced, and she shivered. What if her father succeeded in killing River next time?

River squeezed her hand and she prayed his plan would work. She moved past her father to hug her mum. "I love you," her mum said. "Don't you worry about anything but being happy."

Ally searched her eyes. Her blue eyes looked hopeful and radiant. She wished she knew exactly what River's plan was to rescue her mum. It had to be foolproof, and even then her father would hunt his wife down. Ally knew that. But she trusted River. If anyone could accomplish the impossible, he could.

River's parents were next, and it was so cute to see him engulf his tiny mum in a hug. His mum kept patting his cheeks. "So handsome. I love you so much." She turned to Ally. "Oh, you beauty! I love you," she gushed, seizing Ally in a fierce hug. As Ally returned the hug, his mum's encouraging whisper reached her ear: "I've got your mama. Don't you worry about a thing, darlin'."

River's dad engulfed her in a hug next. He pulled back and grinned from her to her father. "Your father and I are going to get a business deal out of this marriage."

His words reassured her as much as anything. River's father was the billionaire American her father had been so excited to meet. Business was her father's language. If River's father brought in more money than a union with Henry would've done, maybe it would alleviate some of the damage her father intended.

River wrapped his arm around her waist and escorted her back through the throng. Cameras flashed and people enthused their congratulations, but luckily no one tried to stop them. River nodded to the burly men who had pushed Henry out of the way, then leaned down close to Ally. "Ready to get out of here, love?"

She glanced back. "My mum?"

River squeezed her waist. "She's leaving another direction."

Ally could see her father and River's father talking intently, but his mum and hers were gone. With a sigh of relief, she let River whisk her out the front doors and to a waiting limousine. The driver gladly helped them inside.

River wrapped his arms around her and explained, "Your mom —mum, excuse me—is headed to the ladies' room—I mean, the loo —by way of the underground garage, where Sutton will be waiting for her. Lord Kingsley is one of Sutton's closest friends."

"Sutton's your boss?" She remembered the name.

He nodded and brushed the hair from her neck, his warm touch doing a number on her sensitive skin. "He'll protect her better than anyone I know, and our team will make sure neither of us are followed."

"But what about my father? Is your father really doing a business deal with him?"

"Your father's going to believe he is." River's smile looked as calculating and scary as she'd ever seen it. "Kingsley, Sutton, and my father have some things planned for your father. I think he'll be too busy to worry about us or your mum."

Ally leaned against him, her thoughts spinning at how everything had flipped upside down in just a few minutes. She held up her left hand and admired her sparkling diamond. "Did that really just happen?"

"Are you regretting it already?" He smirked at her.

"Well," she teased, "I don't know you very well."

"What would you like to know?"

Ally traced her finger across his lips. "I'd like to get to know these better."

River grinned and easily lifted her onto his lap. "Now that I can help you with." His smile turned serious as he slowly lowered his head to hers. "I love you, Ally," he whispered.

"I love you."

Then his mouth claimed hers. His lips were strong and possessive and reassured her that they belonged together. Ally wrapped both arms around his neck and pulled him even closer. When he gently deepened the kiss, she felt like she was soaring. River was truly hers and she was his. Ally was going to love getting to know everything about her new husband.

CHAPTER TWENTY-THREE

ALLY EASED over the last few feet of Crawler's Ledge and kept moving down the trail. River was right behind her, and she paused to take in the breathtaking view of Kalalau Beach down below and the lush, green mountains above. "I love that we're doing this hike on our honeymoon," she said.

"You would." River grinned at her. "You and your crazy hiking adventures."

Ally laughed and picked the pace back up. A couple of miles later, they entered the valley. It was so unreal and picturesque she caught a breath—green trees, bushes, and even moss climbing up the cliffside. She'd almost forgotten how gorgeous it was.

Easing her backpack off, she turned to River. He set his backpack down and swooped her off her feet. Ally threw back her head and laughed. He kissed her tenderly right above her collarbone, and all laughter ceased as she cradled his face with both hands and pulled his lips to hers. Fire spread through her limbs making her forget she was tired from the hike.

"Ooh, come on, haole, you'll get enough smooching later." A voice rang from the trees.

Ally jerked her head up. Standing next to the trees were three young men who looked vaguely familiar. One with blond dreadlocks stepped forward. "Got everything ready for you, military man."

"Thanks, Quinn." River lifted his chin toward him. "I owe you, buddy."

"I know. You'll save my life someday, I'm sure."

River laughed. "I hope so."

"Happy honeymoon, pretty girl," the tallest one shouted. They all grinned and their bare cheeks disappeared into the greenery.

Ally clung to River's neck. "Were those guys ...?"

"The hippies that saved my life? Yeah."

"You'll have to tell me that story again."

"Later." He kissed her quickly, then carried her through the trees.

The scent of pizza wafted through the air, and she couldn't help but laugh with sheer joy. River glanced down at her, the indentation in his cheek deepening with a satisfied grin.

A small clearing opened up before them, boasting a large tent. Outside there was a table set up with two chairs, pizza, salad, dressings, and sparkling water. River carried her to the tent and lifted the flap. Inside was a beautiful queen bed covered with rose petals and a side table with chocolates, more sparkling water, and a small tray of fruit.

"River? How did you—? The hippies did this?"

"Well, we had a little help from a buddy who likes to fly helicopters." He grinned cockily. "Don't worry, they'll fly it all out of here after we leave."

"It's so beautiful. I planned on sleeping in my pop-up tent and that thin mattress."

"I have good memories of that pop-up tent."

"Oh, yeah, when you kissed me and then said we shouldn't."

He kissed her long and slow. "Don't worry. I'll never say something stupid like that again."

"Thank heavens." She smiled. "Now how am I going to sleep in that beautiful bed as dirty as I am?"

River chuckled and slid her to her feet. "Luckily there's a waterfall I can shower you off in."

Ally pushed all the bad memories of that waterfall away. They were here creating new, beautiful memories. She had no clue where her mum was, just that she was no longer in the duke's mansion in Kensington. They had communicated twice through some secure channels, and it didn't matter where she was; she was safe. Ally was ready to be done with all the ugly memories and create something wonderful with River.

"Can we eat before we shower?" River asked. "I've been dying to try the hippies' pizza for a long time."

Ally laughed. "You'll probably hate it. I doubt they killed a pig to create you a meat lover's."

"Don't put anything past my little buddies. They're pretty resourceful."

"Okay, we can eat first. After we wash our hands ... and you kiss me a few more times."

River tugged her close. "I think I can acquiesce to both of those demands." He bent down and their breaths intermingled.

"Sorry you have such a demanding wife," she whispered against his lips.

"It's okay. I'm getting used to it."

She gasped and pulled back.

River chuckled and tugged her against his chest. "I love my beautiful wife ... even if she is demanding."

She giggled. "Jammy for you, she loves you back."

"Very lucky," he agreed, and she loved that he was learning her lingo.

His lips met hers. Ally sighed and melted against him. She traced her hands up his muscular chest, and he held her firmly yet tenderly, showing how much he loved her. The kiss reached new heights as he lifted her completely off her feet. Not even his pizza getting cold or the hippies laughing behind the trees could pull them apart.

ABOUT THE AUTHOR

CAMI CHECKETTS IS A WIFE to a daredevil husband, a mother to four future WWF champions, an exercise scientist trying to make her corner of the world healthier, and a writer hoping for more time to write.

Sign up for Cami's newsletter to receive a free ebook copy of *The Resilient One: A Billionaire Bride Pact Romance* and information about new releases, discounts, and promotions here.

Read on for the first chapter of Liz (Ally's mum) and Sutton's story in *The Captivating Warrior*. If you were disappointed that the Duke of Gunthry didn't get what was coming to him, you will love this fast-paced and romantic story by myself and Daniel Banner. *The Captivating Warrior* will be released April 24th to cap off the rest of the fabulous Navy SEAL Romances by Daniel Banner, Kimberly Krey, Taylor Hart, and Jennifer Youngblood. Happy reading!

www.camichecketts.com
cami@camichecketts.com

EXCERPT: THE CAPTIVATING WARRIOR

Sutton Smith entered the elegant ballroom with his spine stiff and his head held high. He hadn't been on the soil of his motherland for over twenty-five years. Eerie how familiar it all felt. He glanced at his men, dressed in tuxedos and spread throughout the room to blend in. Other members of the team were performing roles in other parts of the estate. This was River's mission and plan, but Sutton would make certain it all executed perfectly.

Lord Kingsley spotted him and inclined his own chin toward a dark corner, away from the media and any watchful eyes. Sutton followed him at a sedate pace, extending his hand to his lifelong friend when they stopped behind some potted plants.

"It's been too long, old chap." Kingsley pumped his hand vigorously. "I say, do you ever age?"

Sutton arched an eyebrow and clapped him on the shoulder. "You're the one who looks fabulous." Kingsley had gone soft and portly but his eyes still sparkled with mischievous humor, reminding Sutton of young and innocent days he'd never see again. "How's the family?"

"Happy and busy. I am a blessed man."

Sutton forced a smile. Kingsley was blessed and Sutton was the soldier. Destined to be alone and sacrifice his life for others. He didn't complain. He wasn't bitter. But there were many, many nights when he could still smell the scent of vanilla and almost feel the softness of Liz's skin. He would see her tonight. He wished he knew how he'd react.

"The plan's in place?" Kingsley asked.

"Yes. I can't tell you how much we appreciate your help."

"Blimey! To have the chance to sucker-punch that twit Gunthry? The weasel pretends he's a good person yet enslaves his own wife and daughter. I'd give up everything but my own wife and the little ones for a night like this."

Sutton completely agreed. This sucker-punch had been due for decades. Interesting that one of Sutton's own men, River, and Liz's daughter, Ally, were the instigators and not Sutton. He'd fought so many battles yet he'd never come to claim Liz like he'd always wanted. But that was because of choices she'd made. He wouldn't surrender his pride, even for her. It seemed fate, however, wouldn't leave well enough alone.

He shook his old friend's hand again. "Get back to being the esteemed host, chum."

"Right you are. Let's catch up before you leave the country."

Sutton inclined his chin and watched his friend bustle away. If the plan went accordingly there would be no time for catching up. His heart beat faster at the thought of the entirety of the plan. Elizabeth, Duchess of Gunthry, would be leaving with him tonight, although she didn't know it yet.

How would she react to seeing him? How was *he* going to stay detached and aloof? He straightened his spine and reminded himself that she'd chosen the duke over him twenty-five years ago. She was simply a mission to him now. An abused woman who needed rescuing. The thought of his sweet Liz being beaten down and belittled by the duke all these years ripped at him.

A slight ruckus at the entry drew his eyes. Cameras were

flashing like mad as the duke and Liz glided into the room. Liz was as exquisite and perfect as ever. Her blonde hair was swept up with a few curls adorning her beautiful face. Her skin was smooth and unblemished. Her body was lithe and curvy in the fitted, silver dress. But to him Liz was so much more than the most beautiful woman he'd ever seen. She was sweet, kind, had an understated humor, and an undying love for those less fortunate.

Sutton's mouth went dry and he could smell vanilla. Liz. She was here and soon she'd be in his arms again.

No. He had to be strong and professional. She wasn't his Liz anymore. She would never be his Liz again. Sutton's eyes flickered to the duke, smiling regally and shaking first Lord Kingsley's hand and then being introduced to River's father and mother, Barry and Poppy. Barry Duncan and Lord Kingsley were about to help Sutton and River give the duke everything he deserved. Sutton allowed himself a small smile, despite the ache he was feeling for Liz.

High stakes had always been a part of Sutton's life—in his short military career, in business, in the Warrior Project. This mission, however, had an entirely different texture. It had never been personal like this before. If they didn't stop the duke, a lot of people Sutton cared about stood to lose everything. Nothing could go wrong tonight.

**

Elizabeth Gunthry placed her hand carefully on the arm the duke extended to her and strolled by his side into the elegant ball-room. His eyes flickered over her silver sequined dress, perfectly coiffed blonde hair, and professionally made-up face with disdain and possessiveness. "You look lovely, my dear."

"Thank you," she said automatically. Thankfully he didn't expect a return compliment. She supposed he was an extremely handsome man, to those who didn't know his black heart. To her, James was the ugliest and vilest of monsters. His touch made her stomach curdle and her heart shrivel and want to stop beating.

The Kingsley's spacious ballroom was as full as she'd seen it, with dozens of couples dancing to a waltz played by a small orchestra and many more people mingling around the edges. Lord Kingsley and his lovely wife, Angela, greeted them as they entered the room. Liz had already asked too much of her only confidant when Angela helped arrange for Ally's protection in Kauai by an American Navy SEAL. That plan had failed, the courageous young SEAL losing his life, and Liz had almost despaired of ever securing her daughter's freedom, but she would never give up. It didn't matter if her own life was sacrificed, she would not allow Ally to repeat the purgatory that her own life had been.

Glancing back, she caught a glimpse of her beautiful daughter. A lot of people thought they looked like twins but Ally was much more beautiful, confident, and fun-loving than Elizabeth had ever been. At one time, Liz had the confidence and happiness that love brings, but that had been ripped away from her years ago. There was no hope for love for her and to know that Ally's first love had been murdered by James last week had almost sucked any hope from her heart. But Ally was still young and the world lay before her. Somehow, someway they would secure her freedom ... or die trying.

James escorted Liz to a broad, good-looking man and his adorable wife who had such springy dark curls Liz wanted to touch them.

"Mr. Barry Duncan and his wife, the lovely Poppy." James smiled magnanimously. "May I present my beloved Elizabeth, the Duchess of Gunthry." James bowed to her as if he truly worshipped her.

Liz gave them her brilliant smile—she was more impressive than any actress she knew at this point. "Such a pleasure to make your acquaintance."

Mr. Duncan shook her hand, all smiles. "The pleasure is all ours. Your acclaim is world-wide, Duchess."

Liz held on to her smile. She didn't care what anyone in the world thought of her and was so sick of her face and body being the only thing that mattered to anyone. Her daughter knew there was more to her and Ally was all that mattered. Liz would play her part and she'd play it well, until her daughter was free. At which point James would probably kill her as he'd threatened a week ago. "Thank you."

Poppy surprised Liz by reaching up and giving her a tight squeeze. The little woman smelled like flowers and fit her name. She would be a bright spot anywhere. "You and I are going to be fast friends," Poppy declared in her fast American accent.

She released Liz and for once Liz didn't know how to respond. She didn't have friends except for Angela Kingsley and she rarely saw her. James had isolated her so completely that she barely knew who she was any longer, besides his slave and decoration.

Poppy held on to her hand and tugged her around to her side as her husband engaged James in business conversation. She knew James was ecstatic to make contact with the American billionaire. Liz couldn't care less. She was wealthy independent of her husband, fat lot of good it did for her. She lifted her chin.

Lord Kingsley and Angela had the divorce papers in hand. They wouldn't do anything with them until Ally somehow got free, but Kingsley had promised that he would help her secure a divorce, somehow, someway. Liz knew James would kill her before allowing it, but at least she would die trying to be liberated.

"Now point out your sweet daughter to me," Poppy requested, squeezing her hand. "I haven't even met the angel and I already know I'm going to love her."

Liz glanced down at the petite woman in surprise. Something was going on here and she felt like she was a step behind. She did as requested and pointed to Ally and Henry standing across the room. Ally was a vision in a white fitted dress with red and pink flowers adorning the dress and her hair. "That's Alexandria." Liz purposely avoided mentioning Henry, the swine who Ally was being forced to marry.

Poppy gasped. "Oh, my goodness, she's even more beautiful than the pictures of her. I can see why Riv... I can see why she makes such a stir everywhere she goes. And that dress. It's prettier than my wedding dress was."

Liz didn't quite know what to make of this verbose woman, with her charming accent and rapid speech. Had she been about to say River? Liz shook her head. No. She'd heard Ally moan that name in her sleep over and over so it was stuck in her own brain. Along with questions of how the good Lord could be so cruel to take Ally's young love away before they even had a chance to begin? Liz fingered her diamond necklace absently. Liz's own love hadn't been killed but he might as well have been.

"Tell me all about yourself," Poppy said. "What are your hobbies? What do you do for fun?"

Fun? Liz released her necklace and tried to think the last time someone had wanted to know something about her besides who designed her clothing, styled her hair, did her makeup, or which brand of anti-aging cream she used.

"Well, er, I used to fancy surfing but you know how busy life gets." She sighed and then caught herself when she saw the duke's sharp glance. How could he hear her conversation when he was ten feet away and involved in his own? "I swim every day."

"Oh, that's lovely. That's why you look so fantabulous."

Liz couldn't help but laugh at the silly word. "What about you?"

"My life is my boys, my grandbabies, and my garden." She beamed. "I whip those cute little men into shape and they bring me such happiness."

Liz felt the splinter drive deeper into her heart. Boys, grandbabies, and happiness. She couldn't understand or relate.

"I bet your daughter brings you such joy."

Liz glanced over to where Ally had been and saw her striding quickly across the room. "Yes, she does." She wished she could excuse herself and chase after her girl, but the duke would not approve and she couldn't risk enraging him with Ally in his grasp. If he ever hurt Ally the way he'd hurt her... A shudder ran through her. Every day, the vow she'd made to die defending her daughter if it ever became necessary came closer to being a prophecy.

A subtle wash of sandalwood and musk stole over Liz and she couldn't help but close her eyes and simply savor that smell. Sutton. That certain cologne always screamed his name to her. Twenty-five long years and the only glimpses she'd had of him were when he was on the telly for some donation or philanthropist mission.

"Oh!" Poppy gasped next to her then let out a low whistle.

Liz opened her eyes and a vision was before her. Her knees went weak and her stomach swooped. "Sutton?" she whispered.

He gave her a very practiced smile, not his genuine grin that she used to bask in, but a cold and detached smile. Nonetheless he was even more handsome than he'd been at twenty-three. He was tall, regal, with the sculpted face of a man who had been through his share of battles and came out the victor. His muscular frame encased in a tailored black tuxedo screamed he was not a man to be trifled with, but she wished with everything in her that she could trifle with him.

How was he here? All the years fell away and it was all Liz could do to restrain herself. She wanted to throw herself against that lovely chest and kiss him until all the anguish, fear, and despair of the last twenty-five years disappeared.

"Hello, Duchess," he said in that deep, melodious voice that sent tingles dancing along her skin.

"Are you James Bond?" Poppy asked.

Sutton's real smile burst through for half a second and Liz had to lean against Poppy or she would've fallen over. Was he truly standing before her?

"No, ma'am. I'm 008." His accent was slightly different than Liz remembered. Maybe it was a bit Americanized, or maybe it was just a sign of how hard he'd become.

Poppy laughed and then clasped Liz's hand. "Oh, my," she whispered. "If he smiles at me again I'm going to pass out."

Liz was close to passing out herself. 008 had been her and

Sutton's personal joke years ago. She'd call him James Bond and he'd say he was 008, stronger and smarter than Bond and committed to only one woman. Oh, if only the last part were true and that woman was her. Did he even remember what they used to have? The depth of his gaze said he did.

"Duchess." Sutton bit the word out with a bitterness that stung. Yet he extended his hand and bowed slightly. "May I have the pleasure of this dance?"

Poppy pushed her forward. "Go!"

Liz felt like she was back in high school. Sutton took her hand in his and all the years and pain melted away. Her stomach was full of butterflies and the only thing in the world she wanted was for him to smile at her. Really smile at her. As if she was all that mattered to him.

Sutton placed his large palm on her lower back and she barely restrained a sigh at how delicious his touch was. He brought their clasped hands up to his chest level. Liz wrapped her fingers around his broad shoulder, awed by the muscle that was under her grip.

Sutton carefully guided her around the room. Her heart was beating high and fast. She could hardly catch a breath but she could still smell his lovely cologne.

He glanced at a burly young man in the corner, giving him a nod, and then finally focused on her face. "Barry is doing a brilliant job of distracting the duke so I can explain things to you."

The duke? Liz had forgotten about him completely. She chanced a glance his way and his expression was murderous. No! She couldn't risk Ally, even for the joy of being close to Sutton once again.

"Ally," she choked out.

Sutton stared harder at her. "Ally is protected. River will find her shortly."

"River?" Liz was so confused. How did Sutton know Ally, River, or the American billionaire? "River was murdered." Of all the black deeds James had done, killing the man Ally loved was among the vilest.

Sutton gave a harsh bark of a laugh. "Your duke isn't as powerful as he thinks he is."

Liz wanted to argue that he wasn't "her duke" and he was more powerful than the Queen and Prime Minster put together, but her heart was beating painfully now. Sutton hadn't come for her like she'd always dreamed he would and at the moment he didn't seem to care about her one way or another. His words were cold and detached and the only indication that he remembered any of their love was something deep in his gaze. Something no one but her would notice.

"River survived," Sutton continued.

Liz's legs buckled under her.

"Whoa." Sutton released her hand and wrapped both his strong arms around her back. He supported her weight and held her even closer to his chest. "Are you all right?"

"I thought ... River was dead." A small squeak escaped as she clung to Sutton's shoulders with both hands now. River was alive! "Ally loves him so much."

Sutton's splendid arms encased her, and for the first time in twenty-five years, all was right in her world. River was alive, Ally was protected, and for the moment at least, Liz didn't doubt Sutton's words.

He leaned close and whispered in her ear. "I need you to be strong right now, Liz. I need you to act your part. Can you do that? For Alexandria?"

Liz glanced up at him, loving that he'd finally called her Liz and not the hated title of "Duchess". She'd always been Liz to him. His handsome face was so close. She wanted to go on tiptoes and see if his lips were still firm and warm and able to light up her world, but Ally's life and happiness were at risk. She'd do anything he said. "What do you think I've been doing the past twenty-five years?" she whispered back.

Sutton gave her a fleeting smile then pulled back, removed her hand from his shoulder and grasped it again. They started dancing around the room, blending in with the rest of the happy throng. She hadn't allowed herself to look at the duke, but she could feel his glower and dark presence as they went past that spot in the room.

Sutton stared intently at her, serious and detached. He did look like James Bond. The way he'd said 008 had made her want to laugh and pretend she was eighteen again. She loved his quiet humor. Liz couldn't believe she was having such silly thoughts at this moment. The moment she'd been craving for years. Finally in his arms again. This would be the last time she touched him. If there was a plan to rescue Ally, it meant Liz's time was up. Her sacrifice would be called for soon. She wanted to savor Sutton, but he seemed so businesslike, so detached. Except for that brief interlude when he'd asked her to be strong and called her Liz. She shook her head. Ally. This was about Ally. River was alive. She wanted to jump and scream. She really wanted to find her daughter and celebrate with her.

"Ally?" she asked again.

"River has a plan to rescue and protect both of you."

Liz shook her head quickly. A sick pit forming in her stomach. She knew what happened to men who tried to rescue her. "No."

"No?" Sutton arched an eyebrow.

"Not me. Ally is all that matters." She pulled in a quick breath. "James will never let us both go and her happiness is all that matters." James would fulfill his threat of killing her and 'upgrading to a newer model,' but it didn't matter. Ally would be free and with the man she loved. Liz felt such joy at the thought. Giving her life for her daughter's would be no sacrifice at all. She hardly had a life anyway and she knew James would never sign the divorce papers.

Sutton's eyebrows dipped together and his beautiful lips thinned into a hard line. "*James*," he said mockingly, "has little choice in the matter. You're leaving here. With me. Tonight."

Liz's breath whooshed out of her body. The possessive way

Sutton had said that shot warmth to her core but also terrified her. He had no idea how much she'd dreamed of escaping with him, daydreams and night dreams for years and years, but the duke would never allow that to happen and Sutton would be insane to put himself in the duke's path again. The threats and blackmail from twenty-five years previous rushed back to her. Liz had sacrificed herself so Sutton didn't serve prison time for a mission gone awry when he was a commodore in the Royal Navy. He had no clue what she'd done and she'd do it for him again, but now was not the time to get into all of that.

"I can't. You don't understand the power he has." Her voice was begging now. Sutton couldn't do this. They had to protect and rescue Ally and not waste effort or resources on Liz. She could distract the duke and take his wrath. Liz knew her life was of little consequence to anyone but Ally, and being in Sutton's arms was another cruel reminder that happiness and love were never to be for her.

"Power?" Sutton gave a wry chuckle and arched that perfect eyebrow again. He leaned close and his breath brushed her cheek. "Soon you'll understand the power I have. For now, suffice it to say that the duke will be brought to his knees and he will *never* hurt you again."

Liz's breath was coming in fast little pants. Power and command radiated off of Sutton, but she didn't think he understood what he was promising. The duke always won. James would either beat or kill her tonight and she wouldn't allow anyone else to be murdered on her account, especially not Sutton. She wished with everything in her she could stay in Sutton's arms and let him shelter her but it wasn't to be. Even if Ally was safe, Liz still couldn't risk involving Sutton. The duke had evidence against Sutton that he'd kept hidden for years. Sutton had been dishonorably discharged from his position as commodore but it could've been much, much worse. The duke could have Sutton thrown in a dank prison cell or simply kill him like he had Liz's personal guards who tried to shelter her.

She couldn't let that happen. No matter if Sutton didn't love her anymore, she still loved him with every cell in her body.

Sutton drew back so he could study her face. "You don't believe me."

"Sutton," she murmured. "You don't understand."

He kept staring at her until the well-built young man she'd noticed him nod to tapped him on the shoulder. "It's time, sir."

Sutton nodded shortly. He released her waist and she felt bereft of his warm touch. Holding lightly on to her hand he walked her back toward James and the Americans. Each step was a death knell to her heart. Maybe Sutton did understand. He was taking her back to her prison cell. He was going to allow her to sacrifice herself for Ally—and unwittingly for him. He had no concept of what she'd been through to protect him but that was just as well. She only wanted him and Ally to be safe and happy.

He bent down close as they neared the duke. "Keep a smile on that beautiful face. I'll be coming for you."

Liz didn't dare look at him and risk the duke knowing what had transpired between them. James wouldn't allow the media or his peers at the party to see the ugliness inside of him but all too soon they'd be home, alone, except for James' cretins who were always close by.

Sutton ignored James' glower completely, bestowing a wink and a slight smile on Poppy who fanned herself and exclaimed loudly, "Whew, you do heat a body up!"

Her husband chuckled at her exuberance and the duke's silence was deafening.

Sutton released Liz's hand and bowed slightly. "Thank you for the dance, Duchess. Best wishes to you and your lovely daughter." He walked away with his head held high. Liz had no opportunity to respond, which was just as well. She had no clue what she'd say with James within hearing distance and shooting her dark glares.

Poppy grabbed her hand again and giggled. "How was dancing with 008?"

"Exhilarating," Liz murmured.

Poppy laughed harder. "I'll bet." She fanned her face again. "I've never seen the likes of him off the movie screen."

"Elizabeth." James' voice cut through the temporary joy of Sutton holding her in his arms. *You're leaving here with me tonight.* Had Sutton really said that to her? The protective and sensual note in his tone brought a flush to her cheeks that no miserably indentured woman should ever feel. Happy butterflies lit up her stomach before James' voice slammed her back to purgatory. "Come stand by me, love. Something is happening with our little pumpkin."

The Captivating Warrior will be available April 24th.

ALSO BY CAMI CHECKETTS

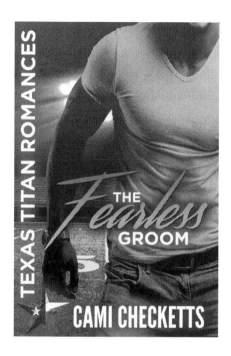

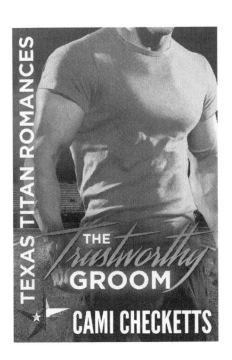

TEXAS TITAN ROMANCES

THE
Trustworthy
GROOM

CAMI CHECKETTS